I0784009

THE KETTLE POURS A UNIVERSE

THE KETTLE POURS A UNIVERSE

A NOVELLA

JOHNNY SCIFO

The Kettle Pours a Universe

Copyright ©2025 by Johnny Scifo

Published by Saddle River Press LLC

All rights reserved. This book or parts thereof may not be reproduced in any form, stored in any retrieval system, or transmitted in any form by any means—electronic, mechanical, photocopy, recording, or otherwise—without prior written permission of the publisher, except as provided by United States of America copyright law. For permission requests, write to the publisher, at CreativeScifo@gmail.com

Printed in the USA

First Edition

ISBN: 979-8-9875618-2-9 (Paperback)
ISBN: 979-8-9875618-3-6 (eBook)

Library of Congress Control Number: 2025906583

Cover and interior formatting by Becky's Graphic Design®, LLC
www.BeckysGraphicDesign.com

*For the tea geeks. . .
continue to appreciate
the simplicities and details.*

CONTENTS

"Tea is nought but this:

First you heat the water,

Then you make the tea.

Then you drink it properly.

That is all you need to know."

—Sen no Rikyū

1

THE MOTHER DROPPED HER basket and swung a wide brim hat on its hook before collapsing onto their grass mattress. The young girl, seeing her mother's exhaustion, quickly sparked a fire and began filling a kettle. In her younger days, the mother wasn't bothered by climbing to the elevation of the fields, but for each winter they stayed in the valley, the first trips of the season up the mountain became a little harder.

The toughest days were harvesting the budding leaves of the first flushes, during the chilled mornings of early spring. Handpicking tea leaves for the annual festival took experience and discernment, qualifications the mother earned after many seasons. While most of the villagers hoped to acquire better work and better things, most of which could be found in the town of the valley, the mother loved being outside in the tea fields, preparing for a new season in her vegetable garden and being appreciated for her skills at both. Working with the leaves was a vocation and it was not for everyone.

Their new home sat on the outskirts, reflecting a simpler life. They moved after the last harvest and before the winter's snow. The mother knew all too well how cold changes people—the clustering around fires like broods, the gossip, and the foolish opinions that only make sense to those cooped up for too long. She refused to continue raising her child amid all the bickering and nonsense. Especially now that it was only the two of them.

Her daughter handed her a warm cup. The mother motioned for her to sit, sharing their blanket, while she gazed out their small window. Snow remained on the pointed peaks as the valley greened. The rivers were beginning to swell, their violent, crashing white waters only a soft rumble in the distance. The crisp, evening air mixed with the last warm currents of daytime, creating colorful skies that gave way to dark, starry nights, as the sun fell behind the mountains and mist settled into the valley below. The daughter snuggled into her mother as they both enjoyed the evening show.

On a route through the pointed peaks to the tea fields, an elder also appreciated the sunset from his front yard, staring out over the horizon of trees that lay before him. The road he lived upon was not particularly busy or quiet, and he usually waved to locals and travelers who were passing by. With the seasonality of the trade, few stayed behind to live in the mountain heights year-round, most heading into the forested valley to escape the bite of its windy winters. Yet the elder did not abandon his post, and when a person maintains such a habit, rumors swirl in the town below. The most outrageous claims included describing the old man as a lunatic, a sage, and a warlock.

He performed prostrations in the direction of the sun, but the origins of his practice were unclear. No one in the valley could identify him from their current occupations. In fact, no one could recall a conversation with him beyond pleasantries. His outward kindness exonerated him for most. Yet his unwaning benevolence while withstanding such harsh conditions only confirmed his lunacy to the conspiratorial few. And since those voices were the loudest, witchcraft was deemed the logical answer.

An enormous fluffy cat with matcha green eyes often sat on the roof of his home, only adding to his mystery. Sometimes, it was rumored the cat was seen with a second creature, but no one could recount its form, which led to locals pondering if it was the old man himself, a shapeshifter. No one knew for sure because no one went to find out. Instead, they huddled, muddled, and proclaimed boldly, with no additional evidence. It was this kind of swirling without foundation, intoxication without consideration, and condemnation without confirmation that made the mother take her young girl and head for the outskirts of town to start anew.

In the morning, when they awoke together still under the blanket, the dark sky persisted. In the anticipation of dawning light, the mother rustled her daughter, igniting their crude ballet. Half asleep, each got ready in their usual way without much thought or effort, before heading up the mountain towards the first hues of the sunrise.

The farm where the mother worked was owned by two brothers up on a crest at high elevation. Their family maintained the property for generations. The brothers wore the same exact face, but the younger, a mountain of a man, stood a full head taller than his older brother. It humored those who knew the family well that the smaller, older brother ended up loving the fields and leading the crew outside, when he hated bugs as a child, and the mountain, who detested mathematics during their homeschooling, spent most of his days calculating at a small table in the leaf roasting house, managing clerical tasks with a small group of desked employees.

This year enough of their family's land recently aged passed a century old, officially designating the farm as an ancient tree grove. The prestigious distinction increased demand for their tea leaves, so the brothers held a special meeting, pushing workers to be extra diligent in the remaining days leading up to the festival. *No days off, big push, unless the storms are just too great.*

Later that afternoon, the younger brother was on his daily rounds, one of the few times throughout the day that he left the roasting house. He noticed the mother diligently picking leaves, while her daughter yipped, jumped, and danced around her. Aware of their tough situation, he helped them move at the end of last harvest. He knew it was just the two of them now, and he sympathized with the mother, a good caretaker of her daughter and their land. His brother didn't mind if the mother kept her daughter close while working, as long as she kept quota, which she never missed. Experience taught them how children on the farm often became displaced this busy time of year.

He continued up the hill to where his older brother was working, who paused at the sight of him. The younger brother handed one of two teacups to his sibling, and they enjoyed gazing over their farm. This was a daily ritual in their favorite spot, not only for its beautiful view but as the birthplace to their deep kinship.

He remembered, when around the same age as the girl, he and his older brother decided to sneak out into the fields one night. By day, boredom ruled their world—the farm, their prison. Their father wanted them to finish their chores, complete their homeschooling, and be unseen otherwise.

With the full moon providing a beacon, they leapt out their shared bedroom window, landing in the soft dirt without a sound, before scampering into the crop rows with their hands over their mouths to contain their nervous laughter. Once far enough from their sleeping parents, they gasped, letting out small shrieks of success over their deception. Now they were free, but they did not have much more of a plan.

In the heavy humidity of midsummer, the tea grove bloomed with rich shades of green. Even in the darkness, the lush trees shined with a verdant aura in the moonlight. The crops, much younger then, were planted in rows wide enough for the boys to run with their arms outstretched and not touch a leaf. The long, winding corridors creat-ed ideal lanes for running, so the younger one, already catching up to his sibling in size, challenged his brother to a race. He wanted to settle a debate that seemed to be escalating each day his legs grew longer. The older brother agreed but suggested they go to another spot on the farm where the rows were straighter. They headed for the top of a hill at the edge of their parents' property, smacking and insulting each other the entire way, as would be expected of young brothers.

When they arrived, each squinted to pinpoint the farmhouse, just a square in the distance. A race of this length required both speed and stamina, a suitable test to settle the debate. In front of them lay two parallel lanes between the crops, before snaking down through the oldest grove, closest to where their parents slept, and the finish line. They agreed the first one in bed would be the winner, and the loser would have to do the other's morning chores. They barely shook on it before the older brother took off, gaining a quick lead. The younger one launched after him.

Down the straightaway, the older brother main-tained his position. He situated himself in the lane closer to the finish and continued gaining ground. The younger brother, becoming desperate, decided to take a shortcut. After all, there was no rule established that they *must* stay in the lanes. He ran through the trees at full speed and did not look back to see if his competitor was close. He tore through the old grove, keeping as straight a line as possible by the moonlight. He only slowed down once approaching the house with his sleeping parents. His father snored loud enough to be heard outside, and his older brother panted close by, but he could not tell from which direction. In the height of the trees in the old grove, the young brother could not see clearly, and he relied mostly on instinct.

Holding his breath, he made a dash through the open yard, under his sleeping parents' window and leapt into the opening of his bedroom. He hit the bottom windowsill hard, and then the floor, with a thump. He heard his mother gasp in the other room, but his father continued to snore away. He immediately crawled into bed.

Footsteps.

His mother was up now.

Peeking out from under the blanket, he looked at his brother's bed across the room.

Empty.

He kicked his feet with quiet triumph before realizing it would be a shallow victory if they were caught, and trouble may be walking their way.

His mother called their names.

Silence.

The young victor closed his eyes and pretended to be asleep. Finally, his panting brother stumbled through the window, hitting the floor with a funny, squishy thud, causing the young brother to snort involuntarily with laughter.

Their mother swung open the door to their bedroom. The older brother froze, still flopped on the floor like a caught fish. The younger peeked out from under his blanket. When she inquired into what she was seeing, her older son replied that he was just opening the window to let some air in and his brother had kicked him unexpectedly. Half asleep, their mother did not notice his muddy feet. She told them to stop fooling around and get some rest for a full day of chores tomorrow. The older brother complied and climbed into bed. The younger brother felt victorious.

In the morning, the boys overslept, waking up sharply to their father barreling into their bedroom. Grabbing both boys by their shirts, he pulled them out of bed and walked them on tiptoe from their bedroom, down the hall, through the common area, and out the front door. As they passed their mother, she confirmed the dirty feet.

The father dragged his boys down the porch towards the first trees of the oldest grove. A path of destruction was clearly visible. Broken branches and scattered remnants ran down a straight line through the trees. At first, the father thought the damage could have been caused by a rogue animal, perhaps lost from a neighboring farm. But a closer observation showed a trail of debris and footprints continuing under his bedroom window and around to the back of the house, where his boys slept. Two sets of small footprints remained cleanly pressed into the soft dirt underneath their windowsill.

Furious, their father roared like a lion, doubling their chores. The younger one, ashamed of the damage he caused, tried to assume the blame to reduce his brother's punishment. But the father rejected any compromise. Both boys were guilty as far as he was concerned, the older brother not setting a proper example. To teach them discipline, he sent his older boy to the fields where they were spreading compost, filled with flies and beetles he despised. The younger was sent to the roasting house to practice his math and learn to control his impulses.

Despite their shared misfortune, the event brought the brothers closer together. The younger showed cunning and honor, and his brother began treating him as more of an equal. The older brother discreetly picked up chores until his younger brother agreed the debt was paid. Their mother, always the peacemaker, gathered all the leaves and broken branches from the morning of her boys' destruction. She washed the dirt off them and laid each one out on the porch to dry in the warm sun. When her husband marched in after the day's work and asked about the leaves, she showed him the limited damage.

The boys were in their room when they heard their father lecturing through the open door. Every broken branch was a loss twice, producing no leaves that season, and taking additional time to grow again. Their mother again motioned to the minimal loss. He roared how the number of leaves was not the point and he wanted his boys to grow up properly. He retained ambitions for them to take over the farm. He reminded her of his father's aspirations to have the family name on an ancient tree grove. He was unlikely to live long enough to achieve it, but his sons could fulfill the destiny. The wife reminded him they were her boys too, that he punished them enough, and it would not be the last time they made mischief.

The next morning, the mother steeped a green tea with the broken leaves to post bail for her children. With no leaves lost to waste, she again tried to broker a deal with their father. She reminded him that they were only young. He agreed with her but maintained their punishments of double chores for the remainder of the growing season. It would burn off any excess energy they had for sneaking out, he said.

As the brothers stood on the hill where they raced that night years ago, each could still retrace the route of destruction, long since grown over but still visible to their eyes. Older now than their father was in this memory, both had long since matured past his childhood anger from that summer. With their shared responsibilities, they could now understand the pressure their father was under back then, doing all of the work they split between them. The stress of such obligations likely contributed to the ailments that claimed him too early in life. It must have pained him to see his offspring act so recklessly with their legacy, piling on an already difficult situation.

With the shared family dreams of their grandfather finally fulfilled, the younger brother wished his patriarchs were there to see it come to fruition, as he looked over the ancient tree grove. The trees were the same, but the stewards learned many lessons to change them for the better. His father was always tough, with the heart of a lion, yet he taught them so much. Even during his ailments that left him stuck in bed at the end of his life, he would lecture daily about what he witnessed out his bedroom window.

Their father's coercion about responsibility had expectantly built character in them both, forcing them to face their challenges. But he would never find out how his boys' punishments drove them to become even more adventurous at night. Through their shared misery, they bonded. They snuck out more regularly. They learned to be stealthier, how to cover their tracks, and these secret adventures fostered an early love affair with the farm, turning their prison into a playground. Only one person ever encountered the boys on their late escapades, one of their grandfather's helpers on the far side of the property, but he never snitched on them. And they forever joked how their father actually drank tea made with leaves broken by the younger brother's stinky feet.

He caught himself chuckling, still amused. The soft golden rays of the falling sun bathed the farm in a calming glow. The older brother confessed he needed these small moments of beauty to offset the stress of being in charge.

The girl let out a howl, and their shared gaze returned to the mother and her daughter. The younger brother smiled at the sight of them, when suddenly, the girl tripped on a root of an ancient tree, snapping a few of the low branches as she tried to brace herself against her tumbling fall. Her mother hissed and looked up to notice the older brother, who was not smiling anymore.

He ambled over with his weathered face, immediately chastising them both. The younger brother stood in solidarity, but he looked away. In that moment, his older brother reminded him greatly of their father. The ancient grove was no place for children to be running around, and this was no time for play, the older brother ranted. But his younger sibling put a calming hand on his shoulder, empathetic to the mother's plight of what to do with her daughter. He suggested during the workday the girl stay at an empty desk in the roasting house, out of mind and out of trouble. Although unhappy with the arrangement, the mother possessed no counteroffer to the broken branches. She reluctantly agreed. This was no time to be difficult with a superior.

2

THINGS TOOK ON A dull, determined rhythm. The mother tended to her work, up and down with the sun. Each morning the young girl followed closely behind her mother, who had admonished her fiercely after the incident. And each morning she dragged herself into the roasting house, a large old barn with a concrete slab floor.

Inside, the space was divided. One side was lined with desks like a classroom, where the clerical workers maintained the administrative tasks, and on the other, a parallel series of three circular firepits in the floor, spaced well in between each other and the walls. The pits were outlined with metal rails at waist height that ran the length of the barn. Upon the rails, the roasters slid huge woven baskets and copper bowls filled with freshly picked leaves. They moved them on and off the flames as necessary to dry the leaves without burning them. A natural rhythm would arise through the circular motions of the roasters as they swirled and rotated their baskets, gauging the drying process by shoving their hands into the hot leaves to assess moisture. It required focus. If leaves were burned in the process, they became "dead" and could spoil an entire batch. Going through the roasting process once produced a green tea; three to five times, a black. While other processing centers used heavy tools and large ovens to bake the leaves for time efficiency, the farm upheld the traditional roasting methods by hand, allowing more control and creating consistently delicious flavor.

The roasters worked constantly to maintain the energetics of the fires, keeping them hot while restricting great fluctuations in temperature. The concrete walls outlining the firepits converged at the corner of the barn, creating a huge, lopsided oven reflecting not only heat but sound, amplifying the yells of coordination between those stoking the fires, others wrestling the large baskets, and the employee or two walking the exposed beams above them, who opened and closed the multiple windows to release excess smoke and heat as needed.

Despite the excitement she felt on the first day of observing the roasters, it did not take long for boredom to overcome the girl. A shallow whirling soon surrounded her from all the baskets moving in circles. Everyone yelled over the hissing and swishing of the leaves, and after a while the commands lost their novelty and became monotonic.

Stuck at an empty desk, there was not much to keep her mind occupied. She counted the beams in the ceiling, then the slats. She took note of which boards looked newer than the others, wondering what could have been the reason those boards were replaced. *A fire? A tree falling on the roof? An owl getting stuck in the barn and ferociously clawing his way to freedom?* Her gaze fell from the roof to the ground. She traced cracks in the floor with her right foot, then her left. Then again with her left, and again with her right. Her eyes rose to watch the roasters. She tried to predict when the next command would be yelled. But, at best, their yowling at each other created an ugly song without much of a rhythm, so it was hard to guess. She practiced holding her breath. Again, and again, and again.

Her only external distraction was her exposure to the perpetual grumblings of the office staff. There was always a new topic bothering them. Today something was too soft or too hard. She wanted to fill her ears with birdsong, not old people complaining. To amuse herself, she gave some of the employees nicknames. There was *Whiny*, *Grumpster*, *Smelly*, *Loud Mouth*, and *Suspenders.* They talked the most. On the few breaks the roasters routinely took, everything would go quiet for only a moment; until one of these workers resumed griping about the heat, the smoke, the smell, or whatever else they could assemble a communal grumble over. Complaining and whirling, yelling and whirling, grumbling and whirling. Even when they were home, she felt like *she* was whirling, and her head swam as she lay in bed next to her sleeping mother.

Each morning the rhythm began again. With the approaching festival, the pace picked up for the mother. Not for the girl. Complaining and whirling, yelling and whirling, grumbling and whirling. She went inside the roasting house, reprimanded yet again for being muddy. She allowed herself to jump into a puddle from an overnight drizzle, despite her mother's reproach, and now she embarrassed them both. One of the women, the one she nicknamed *Smelly* because she wore too much old-lady perfume, took the girl to wash up, muttering about this not being a nursery. She sat the girl in her usual spot and told her to behave.

Complaining and whirling, yelling and whirling, grumbling and whirling. Complaining and whirling, yelling and whirling, grumbling and whirling. The roasters were hot, but it was the girl who was burning, her head boiling with frustration at her indefinite imprisonment.

Complaining and whirling, yelling and whirling, grumbling and whirling. Complaining and whirling, yelling and whirling, grumbling and whirling. In the late afternoon the following day, the young one's mother came in to surprise her during lunch. With the festival looming, breaks were few and meals were eaten quickly. The girl was delighted to see her mother, who knelt down by her desk as if to go unnoticed. The younger brother entered behind her, and the mother held her breath, but he smiled widely at the sight of her as he settled at his desk.

The young girl noticed that he did not take his eyes off her mother while she was there, but he did not seem angry. He seemed happy to see her. When she returned to the fields, he left too. The women at their desks began to whisper and look at the girl, who felt uncomfortable but unsure why. It didn't last long. Things quickly returned to complaining and whirling, yelling and whirling, grumbling and whirling. Complaining and whirling, yelling and whirling, grumbling and whirling.

The first light of morning fought to gleam through heavy clouds and into their window. Under her blanket, the girl awoke to the sounds of the sky rumbling softly, not loud enough to rouse her deeply sleeping mother. She kept her eyes closed and listened. The pitter-patter of steady rain echoed, then another deep rumble, heavier this time, closer. She held her breath, focusing on the soft howl as the skies opened wider. She opened her eyes fully, confirming her hopes. Her mother would certainly stay home from work today in this weather.

Oh how the girl loved this rain! She could play outside, even if reduced to stomping puddles in the garden, which she intended to do gleefully, quietly slipping out the front door as her mother began to wake.

The mother looked outside to immediately notice the stormy conditions and a mixture of relief and grief flowed over her. Sore and tired, she could use the break. But the rest came with a cost: moving even faster tomorrow to fill quotas in the lost time.

Before she could sink too deeply, a scream came from outside. The mother jumped up and quickly ran to the door, calling after the girl as the screaming continued. The cold rain penetrated her nightgown with piercing force, as she scrambled barefoot out the door and towards the sounds. She stepped on a rock, the pain shaking off the last of her sleepy disorientation. She scanned the area for her daughter. When the mother caught sight of her, she gasped. The girl stood in a puddle, deep within their garden, her hair swinging wildly, savagely, as she danced in the downpour. In the drowning, rattling rain, this gift from the sky, so great that it filled every fiber of her senses, the whirling had finally stopped.

Despite the scene, the mother still did not notice how being stuck in the roasting house impacted her child. The young girl was always spirited.

As a baby, her avid climbing skills led her mother to keep her close in their garden, where there was nothing she could tumble off. Together they cultivated vegetables, but more than the plants blossomed. Their kinship grew with every budding success, and the direct satisfaction of eating what they harvested instilled a deep understanding in the girl, unspoken, and long before she could walk or talk. The mother bunched any surplus vegetables each week into lovely bouquets, a visually pleasing gift that nourished its receiver, often their elderly neighbors. When they lavished her with compliments and asked for her gardening secrets, the mother would say that it entailed a special ingredient and wink at her daughter.

But with only days away from the festival and a quota to keep, her current focus remained in the leaves. On each of their walks to and from the fields, the mother trudged slowly as the girl burnt off her excess energy. She needed to run. She needed to jump. She wanted to fill her lungs with fresh air that didn't smell of roasting leaves. It seemed only natural. The young one's back ached from sitting in a chair all day, and she hollered down the mountain road, all the sounds that built up inside her against the whirling and barking of the roasters. But the mother did not want the child to create a commotion. She tried to shush the small voice shattering the evening quiet, screaming and sprinting ahead despite her mother's protests. With no one to protect them, the mother did not want to draw so much attention to their presence.

It was difficult to enforce teachings about good manners and how to act properly, while trying to be comforting about the current arrangement the daughter detested. The field workers always joked about life in the stuffy roasting house, and she knew it was no place for a child to be locked up all day. Her daughter needed to be amongst the leaves, and she could easily imagine how much the young one missed her outdoor freedom. She could not allow the girl to misbehave in ways that would give others a chance to label her disparagingly, especially at such a tender age. It would make for an uphill battle in a small place like this.

But how could she really chastise her little free spirit, her tiny mirror image, when this situation was, at least hopefully, temporary? The pressure of the festival weighed on everyone, she told herself. Things would relax soon enough. The mother took a deep breath, hustling to catch up with the howling child.

She watched her daughter stop abruptly. In the middle of the road sat an enormous cat with the fluffiest fur coat she had ever seen. In the dim light, she could not make out its coloring, but its striking matcha green eyes glowed. The creature studied the girl before standing up and flicking its tail in such a way, as if it suggested the young one follow. The girl stared at the cat in amazement as her mother caught up, muttering and grabbing the girl so sternly she was startled. The young girl looked back but the cat was gone. The remainder of their walk home, the mother held her daughter's arm, explaining, in the most patient voice she could muster, why things needed to be a certain way right now.

Complaining and whirling, yelling and whirling, grumbling and whirling. The adults entered the roasting house as usual, moaning about something being too high or too low. Later, one of the bosses came in yelling, and everyone went silent for a while. She stared blankly out the small window at the only tree she could see. A new activity to keep away boredom was to count the blossoms, but she did not feel like it right now. Some office workers were muttering, but she barely listened. The fires were at their optimal temperature, all red coals and no smoke, and the roasters began another session of loud swishing and hissing. She did not hear them much either. Complaining and whirling, yelling and whirling, grumbling and whirling. She was thinking about those green eyes.

At the end of the day on their way home, the girl crept slowly. Her mother seemed happy to see her behaving, slowly, quietly, appropriately, and did not notice she was looking for the cat. They were getting close to the spot where she saw it the previous night. The girl scanned the branches of a large tree next to the road, then scouted around a wooden bench underneath.

Nothing.

When they came upon the precise spot where the creature stood the night before, it was empty. She examined a small woodland behind a roadside cottage. No movement outside, but inside, candles flickered. Strange shadows bounced around the flames. She tried to get a better view, but her mother hurried them along before she could really notice anything more.

The morning mist hung heavy on their way to the farm, but this did not deter the young girl from playing detective. She could not stop thinking about the fluffy cat. She wondered about the shadows. Retracing their steps back up the mountain, she noticed a figure in the distance, outside the old cottage. A black cat rubbed against the leg of the figure, who was balancing on one foot, facing the direction of the sun, the silhouette only a shadow. She studied the cat for clues, but it seemed too small to be the one she saw on the road that night. And it was rather skinny, with short hair, so not very fluffy.

When she arrived at the roasting house, the workers were discussing an episode from yesterday, bickering about the boss being too mean or too nice. The girl noticed how long they talked about what was said rather than doing what was asked. When the conversation shifted to another incident on the farm, she quickly lost interest. The roasters began to whirl and the usual noises grew louder. Complaining and whirling, yelling and whirling, grumbling and whirling. She sat at the empty desk in her usual silence, not paying much mind to anything, until she overheard someone talking about an unusually large cat they saw on the way home from work, not last night but the night before.

"I saw the cat too!" said the girl, for once having something to contribute to the conversation, but no one seemed to hear the small voice at the end of the row. They just kept on gibbering as if she did not say anything at all. *Green eyes*, they said. *A mane like a lion*, they embellished.

"I saw that exact cat two nights ago!" cried the girl. But again, no one paid her any mind. They continued grumbling along as the day's whirling grew louder. An explosion of boisterous laughter boomed amongst the roasters, and a second joke sent them into a further frenzy. *Crazy. Old man. Mountains. Cat. Green eyes. Warlock.* That was all she could make out over the hissing, swishing, and wild laughing. Then the larger brother came in barking, and everyone quickly returned their focus to their tasks.

On their walk home, the daughter shared with her mother what she overheard the workers saying. She was hoping to piece some of it together, but her mother only scoffed. She reminded the young one of other silly rumors they heard before. The mother looked at the ground the whole time she carried on, distracted by repeatedly re-positioning the basket on her back and trying to keep her daughter close. It was bad enough they were separated all day, and now she found herself spending their limited time together dispelling this nonsense! But the daughter's imagination stirred. As she lie next to her mother on the grass mattress that night, she wondered if there was any connection between the balancing shadow, the green-eyed cat, and the warlock.

3

MIST CONTINUED TO SETTLE upon the mountain, spilling deeper into the valley. Although it was a warmer day than the last, the sky remained gray and muttered far away. It should have been her day off from work, but with the recent mandate and heavy rains, the mother was gathering herself to head out despite the questionable weather. She rubbed the sleep from her eyes as she dragged herself to the window, checking the sky before gazing over her vegetable patch. Many things were ripening in the rains simultaneously, and she would need to harvest again soon. She looked at the freshly picked vegetables littering her floor already. She still had not adjusted the garden size for the two of them and began arranging the leftover vegetables into this week's bouquets.

The sky let out another foreboding moan, waking the young girl. As the mother slogged through the morning ballet, the young one sat up to see the basket filled with the bouquets. They were heading out regardless if there was work. The mother always made her vegetable deliveries, especially in the tough weather that likely excluded elderly neighbors from harvesting their own gardens. The girl hurriedly prepared herself for the day.

As they made their way up the mountain, the mother moved slowly, coming to a full stop with nearly every yawn. The young girl did not break stride, gathering distance as she paced ahead. She looked through the usual spots for the cat, when she noticed someone sitting on the wooden bench, under the large tree near the cottage of shadows. But he did not seem so interesting: an old man, sitting silently, eyes closed, with a small cup in his hand. His clothes were not particularly unusual. Without opening his eyes, he brought the cup to his lips and slurped a quick, loud sip.

Could this be the warlock?

She giggled.

It seemed improbable, but she ran ahead to give him a better look, hiding behind a tree close by. She studied him more carefully. He looked so happy to be sitting there, doing nothing. She slid to an even closer tree with low-hanging branches. He still did not seem to notice her. She shook the branches, but he gave no reaction.

She thought a moment.

Then she let out a meow.

Silence.

Another, louder cat impression.

More silence.

Growing impatient, she picked up a small rock and tossed it, nearly striking his feet.

Nothing.

Finally, her curiosity got the better of her.

"What are you smiling about?" she asked, or rather yelled, stomping out of her hiding place. The old man opened his eyes to find a young girl marching towards him with the authority of the consulate. He straightened up.

"Well, I am enjoying tea with my friends," he said. She looked around. A few birds chirped, the river hummed softly in the distance, but she did not see any other people. Or any cats.

"But you are alone. Where are your friends?" The old man chuckled and gave a slow, dramatic wave with the hand that did not hold his cup, motioning to the valley below.

"We are never alone," he said, punctuated by a long sip.

By then her mother caught up and shooed her along, bowing apologetically to the elder, nearly spilling the bouquets from her pack. The elder smiled, but she didn't notice and busily hurried the girl down the road. The young one looked back only to catch a glimpse of the skinny black cat as it appeared at the elder's feet. Picking up the cat and stroking behind its ears, the old man's eyes narrowed as he whispered gently to his pet, considering the two heading away from them now.

Complaining and whirling, yelling and whirling, grumbling and whirling. Today the problem was too lumpy or too soft. No new blossoms. The roasters took fewer breaks as the festival crept closer, making the air heavier than usual, whether from the nonstop fires or the stress. The thick atmosphere made the girl feel sleepy. She fought with her closing eyelids, until her ears perked up at the declaration that someone saw the cat again last night. They were on the opposite side of the roasting house. The girl tried to listen to the conversation, but she could not hear them well.

Have you ever seen such a large cat before? It must belong to that crazy mountain man, no? But have you ever seen them together, at the same time? Oh how ridiculous, what are you implying? They say he is a warlock, yes? A shapeshifter? Some workers rolled their eyes but the girl connected the dots. She recalled meeting the old man *and* the fluffy cat, but neither at the same time. She could not recall the color of the old man's eyes.

With another day gone by, the festival was almost upon them, and the mother now employed a walking stick on her morning commute. Sensing her mother's exhaustion, the young one raced ahead against minimal maternal protests. They were beginning up the hill where the old man lived, as dark clouds came together to block out the sun. The girl could see his cottage and found the elder on his bench, smiling at the gray sky, eyes closed, breathing so deeply his belly expanded. She sprinted up the hill to greet him, putting considerable distance between herself and her mother.

"Are your friends here today?" the young girl called out, running at full speed.

"One just stopped by," the old man said, opening his eyes. But again, she noticed he was alone. *Not even one sign of a cat!* The young detective knew she possessed limited time as her mother slowly caught up. She asked the burning question.

"Are you a warlock?" The old man took an extra moment, looking at the young girl.

"A warlock?" the old man repeated, and she nodded emphatically. Then he laughed, a great, booming guffaw that shook the whole valley. Even her mother looked up from the distance. The young girl, serious, stood firm.

"I thought that is what you said. What is your name?"

She hesitated.

He did not answer the question.

The girl had never met a warlock before.

Maybe this was a test.

"Jasmine," the young one lied, as her mother neared, still too far off to hear. The elder nodded, repeating the name, but seemed unconvinced. Her mother's walking stick struck the ground like a ticking clock. The girl returned to the warlock.

"What are you drinking? Is it a potion?"

The old man swirled the colorful liquid in his cup.

"Of sorts. It is a very special cup of cha."

"What's so special about it?"

"It is *today's* cup of cha."

So many riddles with this one, thought the girl. *Just what you would expect from a warlock.* Then an idea sprung up for her to know for sure.

"Can I try some?"

Her mother, huffing and puffing, now within earshot, had only heard the last request of their conversation. She shouted to let the man be, when the thunder boomed loudly, muffling her reprimand. The first drops of rain began making themselves known. The elder stood up from his post as clouds gathered behind him. Lightning flashed in the distance, and the wind raced through the tall grasses, forcing them to writhe in a horrible dance. Suddenly the girl was frightened. The horrible dance encircled her. *Was he controlling the weather?* His eyes shined a green reflection of the writhing grasses. His face, perhaps centuries old, broke into a wry smile.

"Come, you and your mother should join me for tea." The mother, catching her breath, planned to politely decline, when the sky let out another, much closer, booming rumble. The rains strengthened as the old man headed down the footpath to his cottage.

"Come, there will be no work today." He beckoned over his shoulder, and again the sky let out a warning. The girl did not know what to think. Her trick failed. Being allowed a sip would have proven his drink was not a potion. But once inside, there was no telling what would be served.

The girl looked anxiously to her mother for a decision, who looked at the sky with a mixture of relief and grief. They were unlikely to make it home before the heart of the storm caught up with them. This man was technically their neighbor, although a distant one, but her daughter already mistreated the old man's kindness once. She did not want to be rude, and so the mother nodded to follow the old man. The girl stuck close as they made their way into the warlock's cottage.

As they entered his home, he situated them at a small table with nothing on it. Rain began to fall harder as the guests interpreted their surroundings. Along the walls, shelves displayed a collection of items, most in an array of unlabeled ceramic bowls and jars. The few items with any markings were unrecognizable. The mother saw her young one staring at the assortment with wonder, as if they were magical ingredients.

The skinny black cat jumped onto the open window-sill from outside, giving a quick shake to dry its coat. Its eyes were a shade of yellow only seen on flower petals. Making its way to the opposite side of the cottage, the cat mewed at the old man, who lit candles in the window to offset the growing darkness of the murky clouds. The girl recognized the shadows. A tingling feeling rose inside her. The child's apprehension increased with every detail, yet her mother seemed to be calming down.

Warm, surprisingly clean, even charming, the mother thought upon entering the cottage. A small apothecary's worth of cooking herbs and spices decorated the shelves, accompanied by hooks on the walls, with simple utensils, a kettle, and a large wide-bellied pot. *A fellow avid gardener or a cook, perhaps?* Her back softened as she leaned into the quirky situation, noticing a variety of cha leaves stored in an open cupboard.

The elder returned to the table, placed his cup down, and said, "Now, this is a very special cha indeed, for it inspired *you*, young one, to make an inquiry into the cup. I am not the sort that comes to mind when one uses a word such as *warlock*, but that does not mean that

I cannot teach you about magic. I can show you many powers through the leaves. You will learn everything you need to know before the rain stops, but it can take a lifetime of practice to perfect."

He looked at the two for a sign of agreement. The thunder continued as the mother and daughter exchanged glances. *What choice did they have?* They nodded their concession as the elder took a final boisterous slurp.

4

THE TEACHER BEGAN: "TEA is an art, a practice of presence—to stop everything else, quiet ourselves, and reconnect to our surroundings. It typically includes enjoying the beverage we call cha—although the drink is highly substitutable—with food and companionship. It goes by many names as the customs and recipes change, but the foundations are the same for those who practice life's simple pleasures. We begin with an invitation, maybe a warming sunbeam through a window or a wave from a silly old man. Whether scheduled for a future date or just the moment right now, accepting an invitation includes coming to a full stop to enjoy the company of your guests.

"You can invite anyone for tea, even if you are the only one drinking the cha. Birds really enjoy tea, as do clouds, mountains, rivers, trees, and stars. In my experience, they have lots of free time and accept invitations with glee. After all, the invitation is for more than cha alone. It includes stepping away far enough from our habitual life to give ourselves downtime, to give our thoughts a rest from business and busyness. Cha may be the climax of the tea experience, but it is preceded by a wonderful crescendo building up to the first sip."

The girl began kicking her legs excitedly as the elder brought an imaginary cup to his lips.

"The setting is foundational to how we begin our art, our magic," he continued. "The location does not need to be glamorous, but it should be quiet and free of distractions. Sometimes places are special *because* they are simple, making it easier for guests to feel comfortable, safe, and undistracted. We may not always be so lucky to have access to such a place, but that does not mean we do not have magic! Tea masters work with what is available and make magic with the invisible."

The old man waved his hands and a flower appeared.

"You do know magic!" cried the girl, and the old man grinned.

"I've learned a few sleight-of-hand tricks in my travels, but that's all this is, a trick. The real magic is what I am teaching you about. It cannot be possessed or tamed. So, all we can do is learn how to work *with* magic, and in this way, it becomes available to us. But magic is tricky, and our minds can be fooled. Focus on the art of tea and let the rest happen naturally."

The young girl nodded, but frankly, she did not seem to be listening; inquiring if she could be taught the flower trick. The old man wagged a finger and told her there was more to learn before he could teach her any of his wiles.

"There is an old tale of a professor who came to a village for research and to learn from a local sage. The sage invited the professor for tea, and as the kettle boiled, the professor shared stories of his expeditions, experiments, and theories. The sage handed the professor a teacup and proceeded to pour the cha, while the professor continued on about possible upgrades to the village to make life easier. Suddenly, the professor yelped, as hot cha spilled over the edge, burning his fingers. When he inquired what on earth this old fool was doing, the sage replied, 'Your mind is like this cup, my friend. It is overflowing and nothing can get in. How will you learn anything if you do not first empty your cup?'"

The young girl giggled at the thought of the professor. Her grandfather was a similar type. She looked at her mother, who also seemed amused by the similarity. The teacher was on a roll now and took their humor about the story as a cue for more.

"An empty cup can offer a promise of deep listening, relaxation, contemplation, reflection, harmony, communion with nature, healing, and appreciation for this exact moment in time. It's quite a lot from leaves and water! But the cha does not act alone, and proper practice includes a lot more than simply what is in our cups. Tea gives all guests an equal opportunity to turn inward. It is a peaceful state of mind that makes it tea."

The rain quieted, letting up for a moment. The girl glanced nervously between the old man, her mother, and the sky. Noticing her discomfort, the mother nudged the girl, who pulled her close, whispering so the elder could not hear. But the old man immediately understood, motioning to the privy outside. The girl quickly excused herself and bolted through the soft rain.

The mother watched her through the open window. Her eyes softened as the leaves played in the wind. She took a deep breath of the fresh spring air, studying the swaying tree, gazing high in its crown. Slowly, she followed rainwater as it dripped down from one leaf to another. The slithering waters bounced in synchronicity as she focused on a tiny stream cascading all the way to the ground. She repeated the exercise with more minute waterfalls, until her eyes landed upon an enormous fluffy cat sitting in the tree branches. Its matcha green eyes mesmerized her. The young girl came bounding back inside, squealing with delight. Her shrill cry startled the mother, as the girl pointed to the enormous cat, finally glimpsing her furry mark again.

"Isn't she a pip?" the old man said. "My cat, Fluffy, the way she sits in the tree like a bird, it always makes me laugh."

"Your cat is beautiful!" said the girl. "Her name is Fluffy?"

"Indeed," said the man. "She is so lovely I could not give her a name that truly fit her beauty. So, I went with the obvious." The cat's coat remained dry behind the leafy waterfalls as she sat motionless in the dense tree. Nestled under the stove, the skinny black cat mewed to alert them to its presence.

"Do you like cats?" the old man asked. "This is my other cat, Bones. He is nowhere near as adventurous as Fluffy, although he shares her funny habit of settling into a favorite spot on the roof sometimes. Maybe the chimney keeps them warm up there. One day, I wonder if they are going to start howling at the moon!"

At the sound of the old man laughing, the large cat leapt out of the tree and landed silently. With a few steps, Fluffy entered through the open window. The old man got up and made his way over to the shelf, splitting some ingredients into bowls, dropping them next to a water dish by the stove. He filled a pitcher with clean water and returned to the table, filling a cup for each. He took a deep breath, and his two guests joined him.

A blanket of quiet overcame the cottage as they all exhaled. The stove crackled, soft rain cooed, and the cats crunched away. *Still no cha,* thought the girl. But she relaxed into the situation now. Her mother seemed to be enjoying herself, and the warlock was no longer scary. Seeing the elder with both of his cats in one room, she realized how silly most of the rumors were she'd heard in the roasting house.

An open window fanned an incoming breeze over the stove, sending warm air to their table. The cats devoured their meal and the skinny one remained by the fire, while the fluffy one came over to the guests, rubbing herself on each of their legs before settling under the table. The close proximity of the green-eyed cat made the young girl feel safe, and now fully relieved, she focused again. Her mother never let her try real cha before, always giving her steeped dried fruits instead. She was excited to think this may be her chance. In the silence, she sat up straight and waited for the teacher to recommence. The elder fluttered his hands as if casting a spell.

"A good host is not someone who does all the movements correctly," he continued. "To think that there are such rules misses the point of tea. But there are a few things anyone can do to work with magic. For example, a warm room when one comes out of the cold is not truly empty. We can feel the warmth in a space with walls alone. They protect us, and a nice temperature can offer us comfort and security. Cleanliness creates spaciousness, a refreshing quality that allows the mind to wander—also a good sign that nothing unwarranted will enter your cup! But more powerfully, a clean table receives without pretense, deflecting unwanted residual energies into the shadows below, to be absorbed and recycled by the earth. These unspoken shifts of the inner world begin the healing process."

He motioned around the cottage and then brought his hands to cover his face.

"Expectations in common society ask us to wear different masks as workmates, family members, and more. Depending on our outer world, some of our masks are guards, like armor," he said, breaking his hands apart. "They can be very elaborate and take considerable time for proper removal. No one can sip cha properly through their mask. We must take them off for tea. Admittedly, without our masks, we are vulnerable. But proper tea coddles us with vital life forces: warmth, water, and kinship. It is easier to remove one's mask when there is a place to set it down. Give people extra time and space to relax. Tea is a celebration of ancient relationships: there is no rush."

He stood up.

"Now, here your guests sit: mask-less, guards down, relaxed, warm, safe, and filled with potential. You have already offered them so much magic in the invisible, even if all they notice is an empty table and a clean place to rest."

The teacher looked triumphantly at his pupils, hoping they would intuit that this is precisely what he had done. But he was losing them. The girl's mouth hung open slightly, and her mother looked tired as well. *Relaxed, but not focused,* he thought. *Oh well.*

"Tea is a dialogue, and we would not control each sentence of a conversation," he concluded, almost ironically as he headed for the cabinets. "We must include the feelings of all the guests and give each their time in the spotlight. There are no background characters here!"

He placed a small but eye-catching serving bowl on the table, intricately inlayed with traditional symbols and filled with biscuits. The mother looked as if she had seen a ghost.

"What's the matter?" the elder asked. Now he also looked a fright. The mother's face clearly surprised the old man. She stared at the ceramic bowl as she asked how he acquired it. He let out a nervous chuckle, pulling at his collar.

"I usually joke that this is my pottery bush bowl." He motioned out the window to a thicket of bushes with intertwined branches near the road. "That spot over there. One day I found this bowl wedged deep in the thicket. It must have been there for some time because leaves grew out from the edges looking for sunlight. From the angle I discovered it, the bowl looked like it was growing straight out of the bush like a flower." The skinny cat jumped into the old man's lap.

"Bones is also a fan of the pottery bush. But sadly, it has not blossomed with any other pots. Maybe it only blooms once every forty years, who knows?" The old man said this in a singsong voice to break his discomfort, waving his hands to the amusement of the child—who was delighted.

"According to the mystics, a pottery bush blooms once every thirty-seven years, if we are being precise!" the young one chimed, and they both burst into laughter at her improvisation. The tea party was taking quite an imaginary turn. But when the laughing girl turned to her mother, she snapped back to reality. The mother looked sick. She lifted the bowl to view its bottom before her voice cracked as she dropped it back on the table. She began to weep, a deep, full body sob, taking her face in her hands. Neither the daughter nor host could under-stand why things were spiraling so precipitously. Through her tears, the mother began to share the true origin story of the ceramic bowl that sat on the empty table.

5

THE YOUNG GIRL'S FATHER, born to a prominent artisan potter in the valley, did not want to be his apprentice. He harbored a passion for the leaves and dreamed of owning a farm someday. His family did not share his enthusiasm, making every effort to persuade him to pursue a more practical path. His father was well established and wanted to keep their lineage intact. The potter's son showed an aptitude for the craft but never focused adequately.

His head lived in the clouds, and he spent too much time courting the attention of a local farmer's daughter. When the farmer found out, he was not pleased with his daughter's suitor. He wanted his daughter to marry up, not to an immature fool. The potter wanted his son to focus on a suitable craft. His business associates could help the son find his way. One of them also mentioned a nice-looking daughter the father thought would be of interest to his son. Although pressure came from all sides, it failed. The lovers eloped to the outskirts of town and took jobs at the only farm looking for workers, run by two brothers up on a crest at high elevation.

The beginning of their new life together contained all the markings of a true romance. Indeed, they were very happy, with work, a new home, if rather modest compared to how each grew up, and a good distance from their families' complaints. But when his wife became pregnant, things shifted. Word reached their families, and the young couple faced renewed pressure to be more financially responsible about their future. They came from respectable families, and his father rattled on about how it was one thing to be foolish about their own affairs, but now a child was involved. Again, he pushed his son to return to a pottery apprenticeship. He would be behind in training, but the father promised to help him catch up quickly if he would just commit.

The potter's son wavered. He wanted to be a good provider. But when he asked his wife for input, she began shouting how she would not give up their happy, if simple, existence for his father's narrow view of success. Her intensity surprised him. The young couple agreed not to cave to anyone else's vision for their life.

As they walked to work the following morning, his wife took long, almost defiant, prideful strides. She loved being amongst the leaves, but her husband could not share in her revelry. After rejecting his father's last offer, their relationship strained. He remained unconvinced they were making the proper decision.

Time passed quickly as she began to show. The wife remained distant from family members, particularly her father-in-law. The potter's son wanted to patch things up, knowing they would need more hands to help with the baby. He had refrained from taking any days off recently as they saved up for the newborn. He wanted to head into the valley and apologize. His father proved correct; expenses were adding up quickly, even before the child arrived. His wife sang happily in their garden, oblivious to the fluctuating conditions.

One day in the fields, an older coworker noticed how stressed the expecting father was and pulled out a small flask. The liquor burned all the way down, but after a few swigs, its appeal became apparent. The cohort was happy to have a new drinking buddy, and over the next week, the two began making a habit of working together.

His wife quickly noticed. She confronted her husband immediately on his emotional distance, his sudden bad morale, and how he was already behind on this week's quota. She called out his poor choice in company, how she routinely overheard the old cohort saying disrespectful things about their boss. She reminded her husband this farm was the only place they could find work. *You better not screw it up.* At this insult his temper flared and his wife cowered. Blood thumped in his ears and rage filled the cavities of his body. His wife whimpered, as she crawled away from him. She looked up, saturated in fear. But upon seeing her frightened face, he sobered up. He looked at his contorted reflection in their opaque window. This was not who he wanted to be. Pulling her off the ground and into his arms, he kissed her. He needed to make a change.

The next time his coworker offered him the daily dose, it was politely refused. He appreciated the cohort's generosity, but the father-to-be expressed he did not need any new bad habits. He made his wife a promise. The cohort immediately berated the young man, calling him all sorts of insults equated to being soft and the boss's pet. Then the drunk threatened him to keep secret the things they shared over the bottle. He pulled out a small knife and again declared that if any of this were repeated to the boss, he would go on a rampage. The potter's son nodded. They worked on opposite ends of the property after that.

Without the help of his young partner, the drunken cohort quickly fell behind on quota, resulting in him being short paid. The younger of two brothers who ran the family farm, a mountain of a man, calculated the weekly quotas. The newly appointed manager recently emerged out of the fields to take over the clerical duties from their ailing father, including distributing the wages. The old drunk spit fire at the manager, poking the mountain of a man in the chest repeatedly. He carried on loudly about the length of his employment despite the uncaring, uncompromising disposition of the farm's ownership. The manager gritted his teeth but again tried to sedate his employee diplomatically, rerunning the calculation in front of the cohort. But the man's flask was now empty and he continued to carry on loudly. *You are getting rich off my back*, he said, and he looked to the other workers for affirmation. This offense hit the limit.

By now, the workers in the roasting house watched nervously for what the large manager would do. He asked the man to calm down and step outside with him so they could talk about it privately. The two walked out the door, leaving the others inside the roasting house. Once the daily work stopped, the farm was always very quiet, and in the late hour, the outdoor conversation could still be heard by those inside. The workers remained clearly in earshot, holding their collective breath for the outcome.

The drunk continued to curse, lashing all the insults he had pent up over his tenure. But the manager's voice changed. He accused the man of being a lousy drunk and listed a variety of grievances, including tardiness, missed quota, and an incident of public urination. Despite these offenses, he was given an opportunity to stay on board and dry out, due to his years of service. But the manager had endured enough, accusing the man of being intoxicated yet again despite his previous warnings. At this affront, the drunk accused the potter's son of being a snitch. The manager told the cohort to blame no one but himself and fired him on the spot. The desperate man pulled out his knife and charged the manager.

The workers could only hear the ranting. They could not see the knife. But they did hear the scream of the drunk charging, a sharp yell from the manager, and then silence. Then they heard the large man growl, and the old drunk began to scream, a horrid, desperate scream.

The workers ran outside to see the farm-strong manager pummeling the old drunk, who now begged for mercy. The workers became upset, pleading with him to end it. The mountain stood over the broken man. He picked up the knife and yelled an order to remove him from the property. He yelled to no one in particular, but all the men present surrounded the drunk, herding him slowly as he stumbled his way out, swearing revenge on everyone, particularly the potter's son. Thankfully, he never returned to the farm.

The following day the manager came in to work with a wide bandage around his arm but otherwise fine. His father taught him early on that operating a farm was, at times, more like running a pirate ship than a business. This was not his first taste of mutiny, and like a good captain, he remained in control of the ranks. He was not proud of what happened but stood by his actions. He properly calculated the wages based on the poor performance. He did not short the drunk inappropriately. And when the man insulted his family's honor, an example was made of him.

The expecting father came to see the manager and apologize for not bringing the situation to his attention sooner. He knew the larger brother to be fair and even generous, always kind to him and his wife. The potter's son felt somewhat responsible for the fight and wanted to reimburse the manager somehow. The mountain of a man clapped his large hand on the back of his loyal employee. *A man of such character should amount to more than something in the fields*, the manager said.

The potter's son thought this praise could be an opening and began sharing his aspirations to own his own farm someday. The brother nodded along but soon stopped the man waxing poetic. It seemed unlikely the field worker could ever amass the money necessary to buy the required land on field wages, even if he had seven more hands to pick with. The potter's son understood this was the end of their conversation and bowed out to the fields.

As he worked, the expecting father formulated a new plan. He identified one way to get more money, but knowing his wife and her pride, she would never agree. Still, he was not doing this just for himself, he was doing it for the both of them. Actually, the three of them. On their next day off, while the rains poured down and his wife rested, he snuck a portion of their savings from its hiding place and headed into town.

A knock at the door surprised the artisan potter in the ugly weather. When he opened it, more surprise flooded him at the sight of his son, who he had not seen for too long, looking thinner but stronger than the last time they saw each other. His son bore the smile of a guilty child, but in his hands, he carried a basic pottery wheel. It was apology enough he was there on the doorstep, but at the sight of the wheel, the father hurried him inside to begin immediately.

The potter's son did not tell his wife precisely what his second occupation was, only how its nighttime hours would not conflict with his farm duties. He shared with the expecting mother what their manager said, about needing seven more hands to achieve their dreams, and admitted his growing fears about money. He continued his work in the fields, but as farm shifts waned with the shortening sunlight hours of the autumn, he spent more and more of his time in the valley.

She felt she could give birth at any moment and had recently stopped working. Preparing for the child, she cleaned and dusted to whatever extent her limited mobility allowed. She needed to keep her mind occupied. Her husband's mounting paranoia started weighing on her as well. When she came upon their hiding place, she opened it to see how much they saved. Admittedly, there was less then she remembered.

That night, her husband came home late and smelled of liquor. It was the first time in a long time, but with the child's birth so imminent, his wife came at him like a torrent. She could not let him fall into the bottle again. She questioned him fiercely. He sputtered an answer, but it did not satisfy her. This was his little tic when he lied, she knew. *Tic. Tic.*

In truth, he did have a few drinks earlier, a celebratory toast with his father. He created the first piece worthy of placement in his father's shop, a small vase. His quick progress marked a victory for them both. The potter's son now intended to make another vase for his wife as a gift celebrating their newborn. He hoped to give it to her filled with flowers and the money from his first sale at the shop, a positive reinforcement for when he finally revealed his new, more lucrative vocation. Unclear how long it would take to sell, he did not want to ruin the surprise, so when his wife interrogated him again for why he smelled of liquor, he fibbed that he ran into some of the field workers in town and joined them for a quick drink.

His wife was not placated with this answer either. She pressed the vase maker for details and his story quickly fell apart. She brought up the missing money and the lack of any new funds, and she accused him openly of falling into the bottle. He protested, but his defensiveness only fueled her fury. She went to sleep angry that night, but he kept his vases a secret. They would share a good laugh about this someday soon, he hoped.

The young girl joined the world shortly after the quarrel and her parents were elated. The spat was quickly forgotten. With his wife's attention on the baby, the potter's son kept up his two jobs and maintained a chance at his surprise. She remained annoyed by his insistency on secrecy but she was too involved with the baby to entertain any further drama. But she did randomly and routinely smell his breath upon walking in the door. No additional offenses recorded. Yet he seemed oddly happier than usual, especially for a man supposedly working two jobs. To date, no new money had come in yet. In the long hours, alone, nursing the crying newborn, her dark imaginings wondered what her husband was actually up to in the valley.

A darkening night sky alerted the potter's son to get back home before his wife worried, as his father poured him one more drink. The son had sold his first vase in the shop that afternoon, and his father beamed with joy. He now presented two more of his son's vases in the display window. The son tried to refuse the drink, but his father quite literally pushed it on him, spilling all over his shirt; the celebration had gone a bit to his head. The son shook it off, although his shirt was rather soaked. He repeated he needed to get home to his wife waiting up for him and departed his smiling father. With one hand he continued to wipe at the stain. With the other, he carried the vase created for his wife, filled with flowers selected from his father's garden and the first commissions of his new career hiding inside.

As the potter's son left his father's home, he took a detour through town to see his creations in the shop window. Admittedly, working in the fields was a thankless job. His bosses received most of the glory, especially with their family name on the company seal. To see his work in a shop window would be a treat, especially since he did not get to see the first one on display. He made his way into the lower part of town for a look.

As work became more available in the valley, the new sprung up right alongside the old and often felt incongruent. His father's shop lay buried in a changing neighborhood. When the family suggested the potter move his shop to a more hospitable area, he balked and said everyone knew where to find him at this location. When the saloons began to outnumber the shops, they pleaded with him again to consider a move but were rebuked with the same answer.

The light disappeared, and the old neighborhood felt different than the potter's son remembered. It had been quite some time since he visited his father's shop, and a general unease enveloped him, perhaps from all the noises pouring out the open windows of the saloons, echoing off the closed stores and empty streets. Once he reached the shop window, an exhilarating feeling overtook the new vase maker.

His father's perfectionism only allowed for the best artists to make it into his display. The showcase, a common topic of their dinner conversations growing up, was his father's unfolding theatre, who achieved or was removed from his prized window display. It was never really the son's dream to be part of his father's collection, but upon seeing his work and name amongst these artists, a swelling inside him began growing hungry for more.

As the vase maker stared into the dark space, he indulged himself with visions of success on this new path. He hoped that the money would ease the wounds between his wife and father, and upon seeing his happiness with his new vocation, he hoped that everything would find a path to work itself out. He even entertained the idea of owning his own farm with a small ceramics studio to create signature crafts and cha. *Now that would be something!*

Heavy doors clanged as they swung open, and a group of men poured onto the street from the saloon behind him. The new father watched the disorder through the distorted reflection in the shop window. It looked like three patrons were being pushed out of the saloon by its brawny owners, the offending, two young men and one old, compelled to the street. All the men yelled and swore as they dispersed, and it became clear they were not one party. The potter's son remained still, hoping the scene would dissipate quickly behind him. Not quite ready to stop savoring these dreams, he wanted to continue memorizing the view of his work in the display case.

The saloon owners closed the doors behind them as they returned inside, leaving the men in the street. As the older man dusted himself off, he met the blurry gaze of the potter's son in the reflection of the shop window. The drunk stared at him as he barely gathered himself, placing his hands in his pockets, before ambling away from the young father. He seemed rather collected for a man who was just tossed out of a tavern. Perhaps hitting the ground like that was sobering, although his breathing rattled strangely. The two young men headed off in the opposite direction, yelling and gesturing in ways unsuitable for children. They laughed, as if the whole thing was a joke, and did not seem too upset by the incident.

The potter's son watched the older man, still lingering, in the distorted reflection, and their gazes met. The man looked away but changed direction. At the casual speed the man was staggering, the vase maker could not tell immediately if the man was drawing closer, but the rattling breath grew louder, and the potter's son began to feel uneasy. Their eyes met yet again in the reflection, and again, he turned away before getting a good look.

The young father now assumed the lingering man to be a beggar and prepared to head off before being detained. His staring at the display case probably framed him as a good target. He tried to make out the direction the drunk was moving to turn the opposite way. But in the distorted view, he repeatedly miscalculated the distance and now the man was upon him.

The young father quickly spun around. He ran through what to say to push the beggar off, when the stumbling man straightened up, no longer pretending to look away. The potter's son met his eyes. His blood went cold. He was looking at the face of his old coworker, the drunken cohort. He watched the eyes of the old man widen the moment the confirmation was received. *The bastard he sought revenge upon*. Without a word, the drunk lunged at the potter's son, a crude dagger emerging from his pocket. A struggle ensued. The vase crashed to the ground.

6

THE MOON WANED, DUSTED in clouds. Still warm for late autumn, the summer chorus chirped and buzzed a final encore before the change of seasons. From a small cottage, the newborn wailed. Her new mother paced, trying everything she could to soothe her child, but the young one reflected the mother's agitation. Her husband had still not returned home and she was *furious*. For months she tolerated his secrecy, but her patience was depleted. In her rage, she looked around for additional ammunition to lambast him with upon his arrival. She returned to the hiding spot, yet again. Still no new money. *What is that man doing out there all these nights? Drinking? Another woman? What?*

The dawn neared when the baby finally fell asleep. As the night began to disappear, the mother's anger mixed with anxiety and soon overcame it. Her husband never came home this late, even on his most foolish occasions. The anxiety ultimately swelled into a wave of panic. She bundled and bound the sleeping baby to her chest, heading out into the early dawn for answers.

The young mother did not know exactly where to look. With her work higher on the mountain and her vegetable patch thriving, it was only on the rare occasion she needed to come into town. In the wee hour, the only person she ran into was a baker. He gave her directions to where a group of saloons were clustered together as a starting point. He warned her it was no place for a young woman to be headed with a child.

She followed the baker's directions, doing her best to go unnoticed. She encountered an astonishing amount of people sleeping on the street, the number increasing as she drew closer towards the saloons. So far, she did not see any sign of her husband, keeping her distance as she studied the clothes of the sleeping drunks. She continued like a shadow, when unexpectedly, she found her bearings. She recognized an old teahouse, not far from her father-in-law's ceramics shop. As she rounded the next bend, she remembered more of the old shops mixed amongst the recent expansion. The sun nearly up, the first townspeople began emerging. The baby rustled and let out a cry. The mother hushed her as they continued with the final directions of the baker. She moved extra slowly now, soothing her upset child as they crept along.

As they approached their destination, the mother finally saw a detail she was looking for: her husband's shoes. There, directly in front of his father's shop, he lay slumped over, an empty bottle broken next to him. Fury reignited in the mother and she marched over to the slouched man. The baby wailed again at the rough jostling from her angry mother, but now she let the child's screams ring like an alarm. Everything she suppressed, all the lies she now concluded she was told, and here he lay, passed out on the street, likely from pouting about his daddy issues with his unyielding father. It was too much for her to bear. She was already screaming when she grabbed her husband by the shirt. His head jerked strangely. *Still passed out, even with all this noise?* She slapped his face. It was cold. She looked down to see his shirt covered in liquor. And blood.

Next to his body lay not a broken bottle but a smashed vase. Crushed flowers remained amongst the broken ceramic pieces. The commissions were gone. His pockets were turned out and it seemed anything else deemed of value was taken. Even the button was roughly cut off his trousers. She raised his shirt to see the extent of the wounds, and as the realization settled upon her, the mother crumbled and wept uncontrollably over his lifeless body. The townspeople began to gather around the commotion, as the baby screamed, pressed between the hearts of her sobbing mother and dead father.

The old artisan potter hurried to his shop. After the celebration with his son last night, he woke up late, and now the shop was unlikely to open on time. It was highly improbable that any customers would be waiting for his arrival, but that was beside the point. His head throbbed as he began rounding the last corner, when he heard strange noises for that hour of the morning. He paused and gathered himself as he came upon the scene. A small crowd stood outside his shop. He saw familiar faces, all who looked awful, diverting their eyes from his. He made his way through the people to the front door, finding the source of the strange sounds, a woman and child both crying uncontrollably.

When she looked up, their eyes met, and everything stopped. He stumbled, numb, as if he was in a dream, a terrible nightmare, as he stared into the eyes of his estranged daughter-in-law. An eternity passed as his eyes continued down the body she cried over. At the sight of his murdered son lying in front of his shop, the old potter collapsed with grief.

The artisan could not return to his shop for weeks. When he finally dragged himself in, the father broke down all over again at the sight of his late son's creations. He packed all of his recent work, from display-worthy to misshapen practices, into a box and carried it up the hill to his daughter-in-law's cottage. The morning they found his son, they both wept, but little was said. Even amidst the tragedy, they still were not really speaking, and he did not know how to amend the terrible circumstances surrounding them now. He placed the package outside her home and left without a sound.

When she found the box, the young mother was confused. She opened it to first find a long, handwritten note inside from her father-in-law, explaining the contents, their origins, and the grief he felt over their shared loss. He described his son's time in the valley, the vases, and the intended surprise. He also explained that he did not want to see his granddaughter suffer, offering them a space to move into his home. The master potter possessed a comparatively luxurious accommodation to raise a child, and there was a sunny spot they could designate for a vegetable patch too.

To read such compassionate words from the un-yielding man reopened all the pain inside the mother. She sobbed as she unwrapped her deceased husband's creations: beautiful asymmetrical vases, bowls with intricate patterns, and matching sets of teacups. On the bottom of each piece bore his unique logo, a signature combining their initials. The widow could not look at the ceramics. It was just too painful. She could not bear the idea of destroying them either, equally haunted by the risk of gifting them only to reencounter them at a later date, reopening her wounds.

In her insatiable grief, she took the ceramics with her when she delivered her vegetable bouquets. Whenever she came across an unkempt area, she flung a piece into the wilderness, hoping they would somehow return to the earth and decompose with her grief. She ejected the pottery where she believed these symbols of her pain could never be recovered. The exercise did nothing for her heartache, but by the time she returned home that evening, everything was gone.

Without her husband, it soon became clear that the hiding spot would not get them very far. The mother returned to her family farm, where she found her brother, father, and a for-sale sign. Over the sign was another: sold. The old farmer, delighted to see his daughter, became even more excited to see the bundled baby. They doted over the family's new edition, and as they entered the farmhouse, the new grandmother immediately joined in the doting, after putting on a kettle. Once the initial excitement settled down, the old farmer inquired to the whereabouts of the absent father. The news had not reached them. Things took a solemn turn as the young mother relived the tragedy.

She revealed they were looking for a place to stay but was met with more bad news. They sold the farm quite some time ago, her family already dispersing for alternate ventures. It was unclear when exactly the deal would finish out, but they already dwindled down supplies, her brother took another job in town, and many of their belongings sat packed up. The new location would not accommodate all of them, and the daughter realized that in her long estrangement, no consideration was made for her in their future plans. She replied that it was no big deal, although clearly upset, and shared the invitation from the master potter.

Her father seemed relieved to hear about the opportunity. Not only would it absolve him of responsibility, but *it was about time that cheap windbag did something to help the situation*, he carried on. The daughter could not believe she found herself defending her father-in-law, but she did, and she left his address with instructions for her parents to write once they settled into their new location.

When the mother knocked on the master potter's door, he opened it slowly. He looked very drained but pleased to see they accepted his offer. He knew there was a long road of healing ahead, but all for the good of the child. *At least she will retain a strong male figure in her life,* he thought.

With a shortcut, the potter's home did not increase the mother's commute, and most days she took the child to work, bundled and bound against her. The extra cargo resulted in the mother leaving early and coming home late. This left little time to interact with her patrons and she became more like a tenant than a family member. In her mind, the conditions were manageable. This was all temporary. But after a short period, her father-in-law became increasingly overbearing, as his sense of responsibility for the child overshadowed his hospitality. Although financially helpful, he routinely badgered the mother to find work with better hours and better pay.

Their strained relationship carried on for years. The mother worked dawn until dusk to save up, rarely went into town, and spent most of her free time in their new garden, keeping her child close. In the winters, she joined a small group of women who wove baskets, and there she learned all the town gossip and goings-on.

Being used to the silence of the fields, naturally quiet, where workers were often too spread out to talk much throughout the day, it soon began to weigh on her being amongst the perpetual judgments and nitpicking, with people who spent so much time talking in circles. Every once in a while, the awful story of her husband resurfaced, but she never revealed herself to be the widow. It persisted being hard facing the field workers each day who remembered her husband and knew him as a good man.

The slander of the town gossipers was too much to take. She just wanted to be out of this mess.

When one of her coworkers shared that a small place became available on the outskirts of town where a group of them lived, she jumped at the chance. It sat much closer to the tea farm, and she could afford it on field work alone. It would be much smaller than their accommodations now but free of prying eyes. She figured her daughter could use some time out from under her grandfather's thumb.

Was it greedy to hope that with a fresh start, maybe she could finally find some closure? Her daughter was older now, walking, talking, skipping, jumping, questioning everything, and growing impatient with all her grandparents' rules. As they neared the end of harvest, the mother remained resolute not to return to basket weaving. She prepared for their final exit, a new start on the outskirts of town.

7

THE THREE FELL SILENT as the mother's story finished at the present day. While she never lied to her daughter, this was the first version the young one had heard about her father with all the gory details. She hugged her mother, who tried to apologize for getting so emotional, as the tears continued to pour out. The old man patted her hand before standing up, giving a deep, dramatic bow, like a servant in a gaudy play. He reached forward to remove the pottery bush bowl, with the intention of slyly tucking it under himself, out of sight of the mother. But as he reached for it, she held on to the ceramic bowl, protesting that she was grateful for this moment. She felt some closure sharing this painful truth today. Something released inside her. The tautness in the small cottage broke, and the elder then tiptoed back to his kitchen area while remaining in the deep bow, without ever raising his face.

With the silly bounce in his step, his class shifted into a live demonstration. He peeked out from behind a cupboard door, as he knocked some of the items together, rustling about noisily. The young one took notice, but when she looked over, the old man quickly hid his face. She turned back to her mother, who looked refreshed for a person who was just rather hysterical. Another clamoring came again from the cupboard, and the girl looked over to see his narrowing eyes just disappear.

She giggled, and her legs began to swing with anticipation. The child's palpable excitement was contagious, and she beamed at her mother over their fortune during this most curious day. The mother returned her smile before noticing a large bird outside the window behind her. The black bird shook its feathers as if bathing in the heavy rains and did not seem too perturbed by the weather. It let out a riff of squawks before flying under the eaves of the old man's home. But her mother's attention shifted towards the growing kitchen cacophony.

The mother focused on the old man, who peeked over his shoulder at the youngest pupil, her legs kicking more wildly with every clang. He turned just enough for the mother to catch a wide smile, amused by her child's reaction, and the mother also grinned as she saw the old man clearly. Then he clanged an old pot like a gong, disrupting her thoughts. It rang softly as the clamoring stopped until all that was left to hear was the wind whistling and stove crackling. He stepped over, added a log, stoked the fire, then opened the window enough to waft his guests with a cool breeze perfumed with smoke and damp earth. He returned to the table carrying a concerto of clinking utensils on a loaded tray. He placed it with a practiced thud.

The young girl looked at the tray with such eagerness, her eyes were almost greedy. But for all her excitement, she was not exactly sure what she saw. Her mother made cha daily, but at her age, she was not allowed to drink it. Her mother's tools did not resemble what she viewed on this tray. The teacher displayed two spouted teapots, one larger than the other, three cups, two spoons, a large bowl, and a smaller bowl that was taller than it was round, like a pitcher. There was a metal strainer, two dishes holding two different sets of dried plants: one of greenish dried cha leaves and the other of small, dried flowers and fruits.

Only the fire, rain, and their breathing were audible, as the entranced students watched the elder unpack. It was unclear who was more excited, the teacher or his tiny pupil. The young one rubbed the remaining empty area of the table, as if confirming her understanding as the elder described. The old man nodded in satisfaction and began to unveil the treasures of his tray.

"There are only a few tools needed for tea, but each has a distinct purpose," the teacher said. "First, we will need a kettle or pot to boil water. Then we will need bowls for preparation: a large one to catch working water and a fair cup to distribute cha. The cha recipe and number of guests will dictate the proper size teapot and number of cups to enlist. Lastly, we will need the leaves. The power of tea has led to many superstitions about how they should be handled, so to avoid offense, we can use spoons. Whatever the recipe, the main ingredient is proper attention!"

The elder continued to explain how we offer ourselves in service to our guests so they may enjoy themselves to the fullest during their tea experience: handling all the chores, serving the cha, and cleaning up afterwards. Being of service in this way serves as an opportunity to remind guests that all life contains work, but it does not have to be viewed as a drudgery. It can be an art. Each little moment counts. Each build to the first sip. Each wave of the arm to pour, clear, steep, and waft, all gather energy into the cups.

"Our first act in preparing cha is filling the kettle. Fill the kettle with more water than is needed for the cha alone—for warming the teapot and cups too. Ensure your water comes to the proper temperature, which is related to the kind of leaves being steeped. Boiling inappropriately can relieve water of its ability to showcase the complexity of certain flavors."

The elder presented his guests with their cups and displayed the dry leaves. The kettle cooed, and he took it off the stove. He returned to the table, filling both teapots with warm water. Then he placed the kettle down and transferred the warmed water from the pots into the cups. He took the leaves, adding them to the empty pots, following with another small pour of water. He swirled each teapot, soaking the leaves inside, before pouring out the water into the largest bowl. The wet leaves expanded in their heated pots.

He explained:

"When we heat our pot and cups first like this, everything warms up to help maintain the temperature during steeping. Sometimes we need to wash the leaves, like I just did, and discard that water into our water bowl." He took the teacups and emptied them into the pitcher. "This is a fair cup," he said, lifting the pitcher. "Water at the bottom of the teapot where the leaves are steeping tends to be more potent than the water at the rim, so by first pouring into the fair cup, we mix all of the water and flavor together, ensuring that each guest is having a similar tasting experience and allows the cha to be enjoyed on equal terms. When you do not have such a vessel, pour tiny increments across each cup, going back and forth between guests, and try to evenly distribute the light and potent amounts of the steeped water yourself."

As he explained this, he dumped the water from the fair cup and refilled the teapot with water. He placed on the lid, repeating the steps with the second teapot filled with fruit bits and flowers.

"These small details not only enhance the cha, but they add to the show. Have some fun!" The master drew the teapot high in the air, the steaming water streaming into the fair cup without a splash. Then he added a strainer to the larger teacup, explaining how it will catch any broken pieces of the flowers and fruits that sneak out of the teapot. He poured out of the fair cup an even amount into the two cups for the adults and then poured the special brew through the strainer for the young one. He pulled the lids off from the teapots, allowing the leftover steam to escape, before wafting the alluring aromas of the wet leaves to each of his guests.

"When you act with precision, each action is deliberate. The spiritual teachings say we can never really know how our actions impact those around us, so we must be meticulous in order to reduce our likelihood of causing harm, and tea preparation is a good way to learn to be intentional and exacting. It may seem a bit intense for drinking cha, but the tea master does not stop their good habits at comforting their guest. For the master, tea is a healing art. It may seem like a great challenge, and that is why many of us focus on the one act: giving the person a wonderful cup of cha. Simpler is better. Everyone has a mind full of stuff to fill in the blanks."

He handed the warmed teacups to each of his guests, instructing them to close their eyes, enjoy the aromas, and slowly take a loud, slurpy sip. They swished their tea in their mouths, exhaling out, allowing the aroma of the liquid to fill their nasal cavities before swallowing. In the silence, they sank into their cups. The rain continued to fall, a new song emerging from the pitter-patter of the different-sized drops hitting the roof and washing the trees. They listened to the percussion as the wind joined in the performance. When the duet calmed, the girl spoke up, breaking their extended silence.

"How did you learn all this? You're clearly a master!"

The old man smiled. "You could say I have been around the world twice, but it would be a slight exaggeration," he said. "I did quite a bit of traveling through my time in the leaf trade. Many, many nights of solitude. Alone with my thoughts, nature, and a small pack, I left a lot of footprints. I also worked at the tea farm up the road for a time. It's owned by two brothers now. I can remember vividly when they were children. I used to work up there for their grandfather, before I hit the road." The cats purred as if they knew what the elder was going to share, and it pleased them greatly.

"I'll tell you a story," the elder said. Then he hesitated. "Is it silly if I start with 'once upon a time'?"

The girl laughed.

"Of course not!"

"Well, once upon a time. . ."

8

. . . A SUPERSTITIOUS MAN with a very practical imagination sought out wild land with a very precise geometry. As he stood on the virgin soil, he tingled with the destiny described in the ancient scrolls, believing himself to be standing in a premier equation of elevation, rain, and sunlight for growing the sacred leaves. The land price sunk well below its value, the evaluation dropping with every prospector discouraged from the investment of labor and declaring the land untenable. The visionary knew the trickeries of Mother Nature, how she deceived the eyes of the greedy and how she only revealed herself to those who took their time getting to know her. The land was waiting for him. Amongst the clouds, here he would build his kingdom.

The visionary purchased all the land they would allow him, far more than he could ever realistically affect. He walked the edges of his purchase, denoting which plants could be foraged. He slowly circled his way from the edges of his lot to its center, noting which trees could be used for timber. He studied the ground, following the grooves amongst the roots detailing how the water moved during rains. As he came towards the deep interior of his land, he noticed something that made his heart sing.

A small, haphazard grove of natural tea trees grew in a clearing. He was far off the road, farther from where any other potential buyer would have likely ventured. The thick tree trunks were healthy and mature from many seasons. The random pattern suggested natural growth, not crop rows. He plucked a few leaves, snapping them and enjoying the aroma. The universe already smiling upon him, he looked to the sky, returning a cheerful grin.

After finding the old trees, a strong vision of bestowing his family's name on an ancient tea grove overwhelmed the new landowner. His compatriots laughed at him, mostly because an ancient grove needs the trees to be a minimum of one hundred years old to qualify, and the visionary was not poised to live for another century. He would remind everyone the magic needs to start somewhere. His part included responsibility for stewarding the first seeds and overseeing the unglamorous part of the process. He did not reveal his secret grove, but he routinely repeated his dream of gifting the trees to a son one day, passing on the plants, the wisdom, and the destiny.

His grand vision was based in principles on conservation. Reading the land, he formulated a plan that would take decades to enact its design. The slow integration of changes allowed the farm to adjust without risk. It would take longer for his business to be lucrative, but it was a deliberate choice to do things, as he saw it, the correct way.

The visionary enjoyed a modest rural life, raising two daughters. His girls were of courting age and preparing to leave him, when his wife came with unexpected news. Their nest would not be emptying out. She was pregnant again, mixed with emotions about their late-life parenthood. But for the visionary, the tingling sensation he trusted washed over him. His son was coming.

When they were blessed with the birth of their baby boy, the farmer was enthralled. His legacy intact, and in the blink of an eye, his baby was a man, married, and living with two of his own young boys in the farmhouse. The visionary mused about his grandsons being the heirs to his ancient grove, even before the boys could walk. The old farmer relished the role of whimsical patriarch. As his son took control over the daily operations of the farm, he focused on inspiring the little ones with old stories, teachings on conservation, and big dreams for their future tree groves.

As the visionary's son gained more power, he chastised his father about the long-term idealism. With all these mouths to feed living on the property, the small grove was not going to support everyone, and his father's expansion plan was tepid at best. The son suggested they clear even more of the land and prepare to grow crops with a quicker turnover. They needed to run the farm less like a garden and more like a business, he said. It would not interfere with the old grove, but with the son's plan, his father's dream would survive long enough to become a reality. They needed more help, more money, and a bigger plan, the son declared.

The visionary seemed wary. He did not like the speed of change in this proposal, nor the idea of more people on the farm, more tools, more labor, more everything. He understood his young son was ambitious, with the heart of a lion, but he feared his son's forceful temperament may upset his conservation design. But ultimately, he conceded the vitality of the farm to his son's hands. Although the son did not resonate with his father's teachings on conservation, they shared the desire for the family legacy in common. The visionary hoped it was enough.

Around this time, the master first appeared on the farm, but he was not an elder or a master. He was an idealistic young man, unrooted and wandering, but not lost. Allowing the universe to guide him, he followed a little voice inside. Recently it had gone quiet, the meaning of its silence unclear. *Did he lose his way? Or perhaps he arrived?* All he could confirm was a cultivated passion for the leaves and enjoyment working outside, far more than being stuffed all day in any teahouse.

When the young man met the visionary, the aged landowner was preparing for a small expansion surrounding his oldest grove. A new batch of small crops around a year old were just planted, and it would take a minimum of two more full years of stewardship before they would have their first real harvest. The seedlings were spread amongst much older trees and needed to be cared for by hand.

The two men walked through the groves, new and old, as the young master noted out loud some of the visionary's conservation curations, particularly around capturing water for the dry season. The old man looked impressed, and the young master shared his passion for techniques utilizing nature's help to one's full advantage. The visionary nodded along, listening intently but not saying much, as the young man shared more of his knowledge, attempting to secure a position in a place where stewardship and care for the land seemed to be worth something.

As they finished on the far side of the property, the visionary propositioned the young master, asking if he wished to steward these plants to maturity. The farmer showed him an untamed piece of land adjacent to the old grove. As long as he remained working for the visionary, the master would be able to treat this parcel as his own. He would be outfitted with an axe, a saw, and some other basic tools to begin fashioning a modest accommodation, which the old man offered to help erect in whatever way he could.

It was an interesting proposition: build a cottage and live freely for the next two years without pay but with little responsibility. The limited duties of a steward would allow for some sort of odd job to support himself in the valley. It would be an austere life but not necessarily unpleasant. The opportunity fell from the sky and would surely give him some time to wait for the voice to reappear. Running low on money, and with no one to contest his inner monologue, he agreed to the farmer's deal.

Over the next two years, the visionary and the young master worked side by side, picking in the fields and building the cottage together. The farmer gifted the materials to make a stove for his new friend, joking about throwing him out for a paying tenant once the accommodation was complete. The cottage stood much more handsome than either had initially expected. They made a good team.

One day, the visionary gave the young master two bags of leaves from their hand-harvest in the oldest grove. The visionary instructed him to keep one bag for himself and to hand deliver the other to a teahouse proprietor in the valley, along with this message: *My dear friend, this may be the last of its kind for a while. I will always cherish that you kept my secret grove hidden.* The young master accepted the task, immediately heading down the mountain.

When he made it to the proprietor's teahouse the following day, he met a stocky man with a hard face. At the sight of the unknown farmhand in dirty work clothes and carrying a sack of leaves, the proprietor thought it was a desperate solicitation. He prepared to harshly remove the farmhand, but when the young master explained who sent the gift, the proprietor softened into a great smile, slapping the young man on the back, while inviting him to wash and join them in ceremony.

The conversation flowed easily with his affiliation in good standing, and the break was greatly appreciated by the master. He shared how his father practiced tea. He contained a great wealth of knowledge for a field hand, surprising the proprietor, leading the owner to share a wide sampling of his delicacies with his educated guest. It turned into a festive occasion.

When the master prepared to depart, he remembered the visionary's message to the proprietor. The stocky man nodded solemnly at the news, speaking in a low voice that the visionary's son was a tough man, perhaps too tough. He did not want to speak out of turn, but he hoped that passionate ideas like the visionary's prevailed over the haste that plagues so many young people. *Tradition and manners are still important*, he emphasized. *The ultimate sign of success is longevity, especially in business.* The proprietor collected a series of leaves from various pots, placing them into separate small bags and then bundling them in a tin. It was a gift for his friend up the mountain, and the young master promised to deliver it in perfect condition.

9

THE DAY FINALLY CAME for the master's grove to be harvested, including the first real encounter with the visionary's son, his new lionhearted boss. With his charge complete and grove picked, the master was instructed to join the other workers in the main fields. Despite the gruffness of his new charge, only a few years younger than himself, the master did as asked, willingly, expecting to continue similar work on a different part of the property. He rarely went to the main fields unless requested, and it had been some time since anything drew him up there. While he spent his time on the far side of things with the visionary, the young businessman had already torn a large portion of his father's land to shreds.

Surprised and pained at the sight of the clear-cut land, the master stared into the open hole that was once a forest. Timber lay haphazardly, as fallen trees remained where they fell. The land was pimpled with stumps amongst displaced soil. Everything seemed uneven and imbalanced. The master saw his first evidence of how the farm was changing, first slow, then very fast.

The next ideas included clearing a section of land for planting new crops. They would make timber planking of the trees torn in the demolition and erect a barn for the animals. But the businessman did not have any processing downtime in his calculations, so he borrowed more money to have lumber brought in for immediate building. Not only did the animals need additional places to rest and graze, but the ploughs and equipment needed for the daily work also needed space for repairs and maintenance. More structures were planned, more cutting, more destruction. With every change came an additional task and an additional cost, and soon the plans looked like a sketch of the town in the valley. The visionary could not talk any sense into his son. His ego sunk deeply into the costs, and the businessman grew more stressed, more irritable. His health was suffering, and he aged faster than anyone else on the farm.

The master noticed how quickly things were getting out of sorts and took it upon himself to talk to the young entrepreneur. He found the boss one afternoon on the porch of the farmhouse, creating an advertisement to place in town for hiring more workers. The first gray hairs shone at his temples in the direct light. The master asked if he could share some thoughts with the young businessman, who grunted but did not look up from his task.

The master began how he knew money was tight and offered a possible solution. He had learned about specialty cultivars from the proprietor, how premiums were paid for cha when prepared in precise ways. He knew the visionary's work in the old grove certainly qualified.

But he also knew that for all the care the visionary was putting into the old groves, it was being overshadowed by their distribution method.

Historically, the farm sold all their leaves, any time of the year, old and young, to a local roasting house, ending their participation in the rest of the processing. The local roasters apathetically threw whatever they collected from local farmers into one hopper to make a cheap, everyday green cha. Simply collecting and sending the leaves to the roasters for processing was easy business. The visionary had confided in the young master that no one was getting rich this way, but everyone was eating. *Everything for a better future.* Besides, he kept the best ones for himself, a very modest amount, that he roasted by hand in traditional ways for his own enjoyment. The master enjoyed these primely prepared leaves with great joy.

The young man looked up and told the employee to make his point. The master continued to explain how the problem was not with his father's limited production but relinquishing his premium leaves to the local hopper. A modest roasting setup would certainly cost less than additional animals and land clearing. It would give them an opportunity to charge a higher price for specific harvests. They could also create a specialty recipe for the teahouses. It included doing more work themselves, but they would have more control too. The newly erected barn could quickly be converted into a roasting house. The master clearly gave the plan a lot of thought, living alone on the far end of things.

The lionhearted son remained unconvinced. To the contrary, he viewed the amount of thought this field worker put into his family's situation as threatening. *Why should he be so concerned?* The businessman wondered how much this employee had already shared with his father and worried if the loner may try to make trouble for him. He went on the offensive, belittling what he saw as a field hand, mocking him as behind the times, just like the visionary and proprietor. Although his employee was close in age to the businessman, the younger spoke to him as if geriatric.

The entrepreneur went on a monologue about using animal labor and ploughs, confirming his overall plan to clear-cut the remaining land. He talked about efficiency, loans, and outpacing payments with increased production; a lot of calculation, likely outside of the field hand's capabilities, he sneered. Even if the margin for error was small, he would make it work through sheer determination. He grew louder with every declaration, and when he finished, the lion rose up and glared at the farmhand as if to challenge him physically, staring down the porch in domination.

But the master gave the young businessman a paternal look, the kind that comes from watching someone repeat an old mistake. He put his hands out as if checking for rain. He looked silly in the unobstructed sunlight. The young boss missed the message.

"For your calculations, you will need all of nature on your side. What will happen if the weather does not cooperate with your schedule? The clear-cutting of the land will not bode well if we cannot trap extra water and it runs off too quickly. We can't control when it rains, and your father has always been very wise about this reality."

The entrepreneur pointed to the well, but the farmhand explained the visionary never pumped his family's drinking water to maintain his fields in all the years so far. It was part of the conservation plan. The businessman's actions may upset his father's balance by moving too quickly for the land to acclimate to the changes properly. But the young boss scoffed again, dismissed the worker as superstitious with all this talk of the land and its feelings, and letting out another roar, reminded the farmhand who made the decisions. The lion ended their conversation by stating if the worker's knees, or his brains for that matter, were getting too old to keep up with the changes, perhaps he should move on. He could use the steward's cottage for a rental space, or perhaps he could finally start paying up now that the grove was mature. That would bring in some extra money too, since the field worker was *so concerned* about his family's welfare.

Incensed at the arrogance, the master could not believe this man shared the same blood as the visionary. But as the lion stared at him, he understood this man could not view the world clearly through the greed in his eyes. He went back to his cottage, replaying the conversation from the porch.

The new boss was undeniably full of himself and about to learn a variety of lessons the hard way. The master questioned if his path must include witnessing all those lessons being learned. Maybe he was lost in time up on the mountain. Maybe he learned everything he needed to learn here. A feeling churned lately that something waited for him down the mountain, impatiently taunting him to seek it. *Someday,* he would reply, and although he did not really know when that would be, it pleased him to hear the little voice resurface as it lured him into the valley.

The master continued to debate his future as he worked through the season, until the universe tipped his hand. First, there was the incident of some damage in the older grove. It did not seem to be the work of criminal masterminds, and it was quickly discovered that the businessman's children, two young sons, had torn through the groves and made a small mess of things. It was nothing more than the usual stupidity of young boys, yet the businessman dragged his sons out of bed, screaming at the top of his lungs, as if making an example of them to his employees. Their punishment seemed severe for their petty crime. As the businessman grew increasingly imbalanced, his apathy for his employees grew worse, and so did the farm's conditions.

The indiscriminate slaughter of an ox climaxed as the final offense. The poor creature suffered a fractured leg, having fallen inadvertently into one of the many construction holes. The animal would have healed just fine, but the businessman did not want to put the energy into saving the beast and chose to grind it up for fertilizer instead. Not even the tail was saved for a soup! In the crosshairs of such waste and blind ambition, the master decided to move on once and for all.

Sadness draped the master on his final payday. The businessman handed the master his wages, giving the usual monotone thanks he gave every other worker. The field hand returned to the cottage he built with his own hands, closing the door tight behind him. He took a long look at his home, still standing strong. He wondered if it would still be here, should he ever return. No more farewell graced the farmhand that day, but he did not fret over it.

Damp and cool in the late autumn, he felt expelled back into the fresh air for a new start—a mushroom spore on a strong wind. He came to the edge of his parcel where it met the road, waving his arms overhead before spinning and jumping onto the road to symbolize his spore-ish rebirth. Freedom.

The master owned few possessions, even after years of living on the farm year-round. He collected two sets of work clothes and a third that he considered his nice outfit, as well as a coat, a cooking pot, a teapot and cup, and some basic grooming tools. On his last day off, he went into town and purchased a canvas tarp for a tent, a rope, and a large wool blanket. He included a parting gift for the visionary, which he gave to him the night before his departure.

The visionary made the young master promise to return someday, even if he was long gone. He acknowledged the unfairness of this request, as if entrusting the family's legacy to this man, but he was no stranger. In many ways, the master behaved like more of a son to the visionary than his own blood. His steward smiled and promised to return one day. But for the fate of the ancient grove, he said the visionary would have to keep training his grandsons to that end.

The old man gave his steward a final bag of cha leaves and a stout leather pack for all his belongings. On the inner flap bore a branded version of the farm's company seal, the year established, and the words *Ancient Grove Steward.* The visionary carved his name next to the logo by hand like a signature.

He confided the pulsating fears of his son's plan failing and their legacy being turned in for a quick payout after he passed. He knew he would not live much longer to see how it all panned out, but he hoped the master would return someday to see their vision realized. The master accepted the gift graciously, reminding the elder that he was unlikely to live that long either, but he made the promise to his old friend anyway.

Fully loaded and on foot, the master did not know precisely where to head next. With his few friends all residing on the mountain he was vacating and his family estranged, this left him, as far as he could tell, with two options: south or west. It did not seem to matter. He walked through town and came out the far side, continuing on a road down into a woodland. In the lower part of the valley, the mountain waters gathered into a great stream. The roaring torrents became louder until he met the river's edge. Mesmerized by the flow, the sound scrubbing his mind, he lazily followed the water, unsure precisely where it would lead.

The stars arrived before he found a destination. He sparked a small fire and pulled out his one pot to boil water. A few days of food were crammed into the stout pack, and he pinched a generous portion of cha leaves from the visionary's parting gift. He strung a rope between two trees and threw the tarp over the top for a simple tent shelter. The simple setup pleased him. A man of the outdoors his whole life, this did not qualify as roughing it. With no work in the morning and enough food to support a few days of true freedom, this was—at least for the moment—paradise.

He looked up at the mountain he had called his home for so long, enjoying the grand sight of her from the valley below. Cha in hand, he climbed out of the tree line onto an exposed rock to get a better view, his gaze drifting repeatedly from her fabulous heights all the way down to his feet. Rains had gathered to form a tiny pond in the middle of the solid rock, unable to escape. A fern grew at one end, seemingly right out of the stone. Upon closer inspection, it sat in a gathering of soil, dirt, and dust. He bent down closer to notice the moss around the water's edge, the decomposing leaves at the bottom, the full moon reflecting in the petite mirror. He stirred it with a finger, and something shivered inside the tiny lake, something alive. An entire world, steeping in this little captured space, not unlike his teacup. He gazed at the mountain, dressed in low clouds, as he wondered how many other tiny worlds were caught in her folds and wrinkles and whether they were aware of each other, the mistress and her galaxies.

He woke up the next morning to enjoy a small breakfast before continuing down the river. He sensed that he would end up at the distant town where he once met the visionary's friend, the proprietor, and thought to pay his only other acquaintance a visit.

Once he reached the town, the master became self-conscious of his ragged appearance and, frankly, the smell. He first located the teahouse and then retreated to a small inn nearby, which included a trip to the bathhouse with its nightly fare. Rejuvenated, he entered the teahouse in his nicer outfit and asked for the proprietor, who was delighted to see him. At the sight of the master's attire, the owner inquired as to the nature of his visit.

"I'm traveling," the master said, barely suppressing his delight. "Not exactly sure where I am headed, but I am following the little voice that I have ignored for a while. I will either find what I am looking for, go broke, or get lost trying. I've only just begun."

The proprietor gave the man a jealous look before catching his face. He understood the inner pang that calls many of us to the open road, and he knew about those who hear the cries and deny them, how they have a way of withering in its echoes.

"The cries echo even louder against the mountains," the master said with a smile. "I almost did not make it. But I am here now." They refilled their cups with a cheers.

That night, the master lay on a proper mattress for the first time in years. He sank into its center and prepared to be swallowed whole into its softness. In deep relaxation, he reflected on how much changed since he first went up into the mountains. He was beginning to view his position in the world differently. He knew a great deal about the leaves, and the town life buzzed with the intense energy of so many people. It excited him, even overwhelmed him a bit. Still strong but not the youth he once was, the amount of movement around him could be dizzying. Even when the strongest winds blow, all the leaves move in one direction—but not the townspeople.

Hearing that the master had no particular direction, the proprietor had made him a proposal. He needed a package delivered on route and offered to pay the master to see it through. He bolstered the offer by noting the interesting things headed in that direction in anticipation of the full moon festival. *A lot of women too*, he had said with a wink. The little voice inside agreed, and the master decided to commit to this tempo for a while: focus only on placing one foot in front of the other in each moment, and let fate steer him the rest of the way. His mind ran through the possibilities until exhilaration gave way to exhaustion. Luckily, the bed was soft and did not ask anything of his attention, so he soon fell asleep.

10

IN THE MORNING, THE master woke up refreshed. He went to the teahouse early to pick up the package from the proprietor and received strange directions for where to find the intended recipient. He told the master not to be fooled by appearances and warned him about crazy wisdom. If the master found himself uncomfortable or offended by the nuances of this task, the proprietor understood his discretion. But he assured the master he could handle it, and this would only add a chapter to his adventure.

The proprietor sponsored a cousin who was a monk, *of sorts*. Usually when the teahouse hummed low on customers, he would sneak off to bring his cousin a care package to support his spiritual journey. The monk would be relying on another shipment to arrive soon. With the full moon festival gathering travelers from all directions, the teahouse was unusually busy. He could use the extra cash to keep sponsoring his cousin financially, rather than expending his generosity hand delivering the offering himself, as he usually did. It seemed like a noble venture and also seemed positioned directly on the master's proposed course. He agreed. *Good luck!*

Additional instructions were given by the proprietor: firstly, to travel only by day to avoid getting lost or missing the temple marker, a large hand-painted stone alongside the trail. The markings on the stone changed every time it rained, so he could not say precisely what the markings would look like. But once the large stone was located, find the smaller path away from the main trail. Keep going further than feels correct; you will not see it until it is upon you. Once you see the temple, move slowly and hold out the package. Wait for a few minutes, keeping it outstretched, and softly chant the phrase "mountains and rivers." If no one appears, leave it in the temple entrance out of the way of rain or animals and move on. The proprietor could not precisely remember the temple location, so he repeated to go slowly and be mindful of the painted stone.

Over the hill and into the next woodland, the master carried the package in his stout pack. He suffered under its weight and questioned if it were not a box of small bricks or solid clay. He replayed the conversation, for it was unclear precisely when the trick was played, whether in his mind with false expectations or if the sly shop owner having forged the deal prior to acknowledging this particular detail of their exchange. But the master now agonized from the misconception he would be delivering a lightweight bag of cha leaves on behalf of the teahouse owner.

Here, carry this bag of rocks to ensure you go slowly, the master groaned. The task was simple enough, whether religious, superstitious, or otherwise, so the master did not inquire of any more details at the time. Now, perspiring profusely, he was failing to gauge precisely how far he had walked with his additional cargo. His pack already fully loaded, he recalculated his hauling rate with every heavy step, as he slowed until dropping on a wide boulder to gather himself.

He watched the sweat drip from his nose and fall onto the blackened stone he sat upon. The salty fluid rubbed the soot and continued to fall to the ground. Another drip, another streak. He shook the beads from his brow. A saline shower splashed the rock and trickled black down to the forest floor. He looked at the streaks, when suddenly he realized it was not dirt at all. The black was charcoal. He stood up to find his trousers covered in black dust. He stood back and looked at the stone, his seated imprint fading a larger mural. The symbols were illegible. He licked a finger and ran it across the rock, confirming the pattern as man-made when it smeared. He looked to the ground, and indeed, a small trail led away from the main crossway, deeper into the forest.

Renewed at the signs of his mission being complete, the master took the package out of his pack and carried it down the narrower causeway. He came upon a stone that looked like it had been carved, something long since destroyed, leaving only a base of chiseled edges. As he continued through the tangled forest, an even smaller path led out under the branches of a large willow tree, its leaves draping until tickling the moss below.

Deep in the wilds, he understood why the proprietor insisted he only travel by day. As he came out from under the hanging branches of the willow tree, an old temple emerged, invisible from behind the green curtain of leaves and nonexistent to the main trails. The ancient structure sat ruined in many places. Looking into the main doorway, light shone its way through a hole in the roof. Despite the dilapidated appearance, signs of life dotted the temple, although few. The entrance looked swept, and distinctly human-sized paths were blazed through the overgrowth.

The master stared, amazed at the structure so secretly tucked away. He would never have discovered it without the proprietor's mission. Struck with awe of such covert beauty, he placed the package down to give the temple a better look. He walked up the mossy stairs, entranced by the delicate carvings on its pillars and archways. The small temple likely supported only a few devotees at most.

A sound rustled behind him, then on his right. The rustling disoriented him, and he fell backwards down the few stairs, landing on the forest floor. The noises stopped, but he felt eyes gawking at him. Suddenly, a figure leapt onto the temple steps directly in front of him. Startled, the master tried to recall the procedure detailed by the proprietor, but he did not have the package. His mind drew a blank. In the cast shadow of the temple archways, the face remained hidden as a booming voice said, "You got my stash?"

Flummoxed, the master rose to his feet, but he did not get the words out before the voice boomed again, "You heard me! Where is the stash?" A face appeared from the shadow to reveal a graying man around the proprietor's age, long-haired, bearded, and in ragged clothes. His wild eyes glared at the master, before looking over his shoulder, as if someone else may be watching them. The man crouched down, and the master followed, as if wary of some unseen force hunting them. Then the face changed on the old man.

"I will ask you one more time. You got my stash? I need a supply to my stash, man." The master looked at the bearded man with such confusion, he let out a nervous laugh as he reached back for the package. He held it out to the bearded character, who snatched it aggressively before raising it over his head, laughing maniacally, yelling, "My staaaassshhh! HAHA!"

His face softened as his laughing ceased, and he turned a loving gaze towards the master.

"Thank you. Thank you so much, my new friend. I am so grateful you did this on behalf of my cousin. I have been waiting for you. Come, come inside." The bearded man quickly hurried into the dilapidated temple. The master put his pack back on and slowly followed the odd man.

"You knew I was coming?" asked the master, and the longhair nodded matter-of-factly. *How? I only accepted this mission a few hours ago and came directly here.*

"It was unclear if it would be today that our fates would collide. But I prayed it would be sooner than later."

The mystical words stirred the master. He knew stories of sages, witches, oracles—those who could foresee the future, cast spells, and more, tucked away in the forest. *A monk. . . of sorts.* Inside, things were not as gruff as their outer appearance. He tried to follow the mystic, but his focus remained on his footing, trying not to trip over the collection of stones, bark, and papers scattered along the floor.

"How did you know I was coming?" The master pressed the mystic again, who only smiled at his guest but did not answer the question. Instead, he walked straight through the temple and out the backside into a garden. A tea hut sat on the far end of the courtyard, as they weaved through ill-mannered orchards. When they reached the hut, a small, well-manicured vegetable garden appeared, a reserved area in high order amongst the forest's reclamation of the temple. The hermit led him inside, and the master found himself in the man's home. The center, which would have normally housed only a small space to warm a kettle on coals, contained a makeshift firepit with a large copper bowl. A hole in the center of the roof relieved the smoke, similar to a yurt. The master reserved his surprise everything was not covered in soot. On the contrary, the confined space was immaculately maintained, even by townspeople standards.

The mystic pulled out a small cushion for the master to sit on and stoked the remnant coals left over in the firepit. He situated the package just so and squealed with delight at the sight of it. He turned back to the master.

"So, are you ready for your initiation?" He motioned for the master to take a seat. The master was reaching his capacity for mystery. He took a deep breath, and from behind his furrowed brow, he began to push back when the mystic bellowed, "YES OR NO?!"

11

THEIR EYES MET IN an intense stare. Neither looked away as they took measure of each other. The mystic narrowed his eyes and then opened them wide. The master did not look away. It seemed they would be locked in perpetuity when the mystic's face cracked, his shoulders began to shake, and then his whole body, until finally, his voice echoed against the garden walls and rang across the courtyard into the temple, scattering the birds with boisterous laughter.

"Okay, that's enough theatrics," he said through his derived merriment. "Thanks for playing along. I don't get a lot of visitors." The master stared at the stranger, and the mystic continued an explanation.

"I worried the full moon festival lined up with my cousin's visitations. I've been unsure how long I would have to wait out his next opportunity to see me, so I've been rationing like crazy! I am very grateful you are here. I have been patiently waiting, hoping to see my cousin or a messenger like yourself." He began to unwrap the package, doing so with great care not to tear the outer paper. Inside contained a bag of flour, another of rice, a large flat stone, a bottle of ink, and a tin of cha leaves.

Literally carrying rocks! The bearded man picked up the food rations and stacked them in a corner, but his excitement focused on the paper, ink, and the flat stone. He took the items in hand and, as if forgetting the master was present at all, walked out of the hut towards the temple. The master, unsure of what to do, dropped his pack and followed the man out. They walked through a different side entrance and within the temple walls sat a collection of stones, pieces of bark, and old scraps of the same paper as the proprietor's package, each with symbols written on them, some in charcoal, others ink. Most of them were short, but a few were extensive. The mystic placed the ink on a small altar next to a group of empty jars of the same shape.

"I hope you don't find it disrespectful that I set up in the temple. It's such a beautiful space."

"What is this place? Are you a monk?" the master asked.

"No, not exactly," the mystic said. "I first came out here to escape the city. Literally. I came out here to stop myself from smoking opium. I loved it too much, but I hit the bottom hard enough to see myself clearly. And man, was I ugly! So, I told my cousin that I was coming out here. Only him. I knew that I should let someone know where I was going, just in case. I had heard about hermits as a kid and I always thought it sounded curious, but I wasn't very spiritual. I just wanted to live in the woods without a job. It worked because I don't have the urge to use the drugs anymore, but I miss the rush of the secrecy, you know? Now I am grateful for rations of rice brought by my cousin and the occasional villagers. I'm indebted to their support. Rice is my stash now."

The master understood well enough. Spiritual hermits were not new to him, those who choose to seek enlightenment away from the noises and distractions of integrated life. The appeal for solitude in the forest was clear, but the disheveled living quarters offered a stark contrast to the romantic view.

"I was told there was a temple out here," the hermit continued, "so I came looking for it. I was also told that there was a hermit monk who lived here. I thought maybe he could help me find my way. I mean, at least he was doing the thing I was thinking about trying. I came out, but I never spoke to the monk."

The hermit proceeded to tell the master the gruesome story of finding the monk's deceased body in the temple. The sight of the corpse terrified him, and unsure what he should do, he ran back to the nearest town to tell someone, anyone. But no one knew the hermit monk, and most people did not even know there was a temple in the forest. The few people he did know, upon seeing the crazed look on his face, thought he was suffering from some sort of opium withdrawal symptoms. He went to another small temple within the village, but he faced similar responses: *What monk, what temple, and when was the last time you smoked?*

The man became so upset he went to find his cousin. When the proprietor saw him looking this way, he knew help was needed, either with suffering from his addiction or whatever madness cursed him now. He agreed to accompany the madman back into the woods.

As they retraced his steps, torches in tow, the proprietor's cousin grew worse. They stopped so he could vomit, and he mumbled incessantly. But he did not ask for any drugs to stop his pain, and he remained very focused. Whatever he was going through, it was a step forward. When they finally reached the dilapidated temple entrance, the proprietor sighed. At least this part of the story was true. Then they came upon the body of the monk. The horrid sight came with the relief of knowing his cousin did not go insane. Familiarity with local customs led them to cremate the body, and then they built a small stupa out of natural stones to honor his memory, pouring the ashes inside.

The hermit pointed to the memorial at the corner of the temple, opposite where the master stood.

"I felt so weird about just leaving the place after that. I found it and who knows how long it would have survived without me. But, as you can probably see, I have few restoration skills, forced to let the forest reclaim a lot of it. It's not destined to be a temple again. I am only here to extend the lifespan and the utility of its ancient builders. No need to add to it. The rough appearance also keeps away temple robbers."

"How did you know I was not a robber?" the master inquired.

"Well, I heard you coming. Living out here turns you into a fox." He smiled, placing his hands on his head like giant ears. "Also, that's my cousin's wrapping paper. Always the same, so I can use it for my poems." He motioned to his collection of bark, stones, and wrapping papers, each etched with unique markings but not any recognizable language.

"There are spiritual teachings that tell us to forgo books and scripture so that everything we utilize for our decision-making comes from experience. I cannot read, so I liked hearing that: the idea that you don't need any special skills to become enlightened. I have taken to writing things down in my own way. It helps my meditation practice, but I know these poems are useless to anyone else. That's why I only draw in this ink or charcoal. Someday, the temple will collapse, and all the pieces will return to the earth. My lessons will just seep into the ground but not poison it. Just like us."

The master agreed, adding how everything properly made to celebrate tea is comprised of organic materials. It is a lesson in impermanence, that each element will ultimately return to ash and dust, only to come back again as leaves, rain, and clay.

The hermit smiled and placed the newly acquired ink bottle and paper in their places for the appropriate moment. He took the large stone in his hands, grinning widely.

"I am sorry you were asked to carry this. My cousin knows I like a good rock for drawing. The stones around here are mostly round. This flat one is quite lovely." He placed it gently by the ink.

"Can I offer you a cup of cha? I would not want to keep you too long if you have other plans, but I always enjoy the company." Having nowhere else to be, the master obliged. They returned to the hut and the hermit placed a kettle over the open fire.

As the water boiled, the men exchanged their affections for cha. At the sight of the monk's gleaming eyes, the master pulled out the visionary's gift, handing the sack to the hermit for inspection. He sniffed the leaves but did not touch them, asking the master if he studied tea as a spiritual path. The master shook his head, interested in what he meant.

"In some traditions, tea is practiced as a path to spiritual awakening," the hermit shared. "They say, the more open your spirit, the more likely you are to replenish yourself completely with a simple cup of tea. When you are so open that you can take your tea anywhere, that is when you have the perfect cup. That is when all the world is a teahouse, a monastery, heaven on earth. One becomes a master, the invitation to accept peace omnipresent in the wind, sun, and moon."

The master pondered the idea, but the hermit continued, while he filled a large teapot with a lavish helping of leaves.

"What I have really learned out here is that most of our problems are fake. They only exist in the mind. People will say, 'Oh, just because it's in the mind, it does not exist? Fear is real, fear only exists in the mind.' But things do not manifest a certain way simply because we think them. Thinking is not action. It may lead to action, but it is not action alone. You can think about being warm, but that does not make a fire."

The master, quickly growing fond of his new friend, agreed. *Crazy wisdom, indeed.* He added there was no more direct satisfaction than chopping wood or focusing during cha ceremony and getting the intended flavor profile just right.

"Direct experience keeps us in the present moment," the hermit confirmed. "It matters less what the situation is and more about bringing the person back into themselves, to go from spectator to actor in their show. Depression is living in the past and anxiousness is living in the future. Both can be remedied with a warm cup that brings one back to the here and now."

He poured out a thick, golden liquor from the pot, distributing it evenly between two clay cups.

"With a proper attitude, the unique beauty of each cup keeps us curious. Each day is a novel offering. Do we grace ourselves with the natural gifts of grounding energy under our feet, sun on our faces, and fresh air in our lungs? Do we remind ourselves that every day is a unique blend of colors, smells, and sounds for our enjoyment if we seek it? Can we create a small air of mystery to encourage keeping inquisitive about life's unknowns? Curiosity is what keeps us from becoming entrenched in our ways. It is what keeps us rethinking and reflecting on how we live, to dare to think if there is another, better way to be and how to spend our time, energy, and resources—connecting, being deliberate, moving slowly but purposefully, engaging ourselves nonverbally, cultivating peace. We can take these qualities into each of our tasks as a daily meditation. Then life becomes a meditation."

It grew increasingly clear the hermit had not entertained any guests or anyone to speak with in a long time. The master remained silent, allowing the hermit to continue sharing his thoughts.

"Tea is like meditation. It should leave us more refreshed than when we walked in, do you agree? That is a true sign of healing. There is no reason why we must discard our state of peacefulness when we leave the cushion."

He handed the master a cup. The smell was strong, a clear sign of the hermit's generous helping. The master did not mind.

"In a perfect world, it would be lovely to take a break whenever we felt ourselves retreating from our present state of peace. Out here, I can do that. Just sit back down. But most of us do not have such a luxury, and so we must practice staying peaceful in between our meditation sessions."

"Or in between our tea times," the master rang. The two laughed at the honest assessment. They sank into their cups, and the mind of the master slowed and resumed its peaceful state of being. With a clear head, he finally remembered the phrase from the proprietor he could not recall upon his funny introduction to the hermit.

"What is the significance of *mountains and rivers*? Your cousin told me to chant it like a password, but you know what actually happened instead."

The hermit looked tickled.

"It's one of my favorite sutras, a sign that you were a friend. 'Mountains are mountains, and rivers are rivers. Then mountains are *not* mountains, and rivers are *not* rivers. But then, mountains are mountains, and rivers are rivers.'"

The master nodded, but the look on his face must have portrayed his lack of understanding.

"It's a funny one," the hermit admitted. "But this is my understanding of it: First, we see things without really seeing them. A mountain is just a mountain, a river is just a river. We can see them with our eyes, but they don't have a deeper meaning. Then, as we advance in our spiritual practice, everything becomes alive! We see not just a mountain but a home for the plants and animals. You can grasp the story of time as the mountain returns to dust. The river is not one thing but countless droplets all together. But we must be careful not to get lost in the wonderful complexity of the individual pieces. We must take life as a whole. At that point, we do not separate ourselves from our surroundings. But we are humans, not mountains. They do not respond to our wishes or even our names. They return to being mountains and rivers. *But we are not the same.*"

This explanation resonated with the master greatly. He added that in order to live in this full, holistic way, he resigned control of his fate, sharing his credo about putting one foot in front of the other and listening to the little voice.

"You are doing it, my friend. Wisdom continues to outgrow us as individuals, but we can tap into it if we choose to listen more and speak less," the hermit said. "We need solitude to find the quiet sometimes, but it's worth the sacrifice."

Then the hermit suddenly bolted upright, mumbling something about having an idea, and tapped the master to follow as he shot out of the hut. He scurried into the temple and grabbed the large flat stone from the proprietor's most recent package.

The master scarcely made it into the temple when the hermit appeared in the doorway with the rock, raising it overhead. The master leapt to the side, narrowly avoiding the hermit and the stone as he smashed it on the ground. It broke cleanly into three pieces, and the hermit grabbed each of them before hurrying back into the temple without a word.

As the master followed him inside, the hermit opened the ink bottle and dropped the smallest of the three pieces onto the altar. He removed a piece of cloth and rubbed the stone vigorously. Then he took a hand-made brush of sticks and grasses, dipping it in the ink bottle, and painted a circle on the chipped stone. The stroke, smooth and symmetrical, received three small lines in the center. He handed the stone to the master.

"You carried this rock far enough, so it's only fitting you keep a piece of it. Trust yourself. Never stop listening to the little voice."

"I followed that voice all over the countryside," said the elder to the mother and young girl. "I followed it to the salted shores and through the mountains again. But I was chasing," he said, grasping at the air in front of him. He stood up and pulled a small stone from the cupboard. He placed it on the table, the faint marking of the circle and lines still visible. The mother and daughter gawked at the stone, as if observing a religious artifact. They remained entranced by the storyteller, who began refilling their cups. "I floated so far I began to think I was destined to get lost for good. So, I started back towards the one place I still felt was my home, when one day, most unexpectedly, everything changed. I fell in love with a river."

12

ON A MOST UNEXPECTED day, the master relaxed at a teahouse of his preferred style, in a port city along the river, where there were as many languages as people. It was a bustling place, the kind that would have over-whelmed him as a younger man. But now, he remained collected amongst the conflicting energies, his inner quiet often reflected on his calm face. The little voice had gone quiet again recently and it was unclear what life was plotting for him next.

A woman came over to his table, announced herself as his server, and asked for his order. She looked at him closer and made a recommendation. He nodded. A fine choice. Then she said, "You got an interesting face. You cloud folk?"

Her directness confused him, and he could not place the foreign accent, but he took her in complete view, a middle-aged woman with plain features. Her appearance was not as colorful as her demeanor.

"Cloud folk?" he repeated.

"Yeah, you know, people who live high on the mountain. They live amongst the clouds or at least that is how it looks from down here. You look like one of those meditation guys they draw sitting on clouds."

"Is that a good thing?"

"Sure, you are *so* exotic." She rolled her eyes, and his puzzlement continued, but she seemed to be teasing him, touching his shoulder and coming close to his face as she said it. *How forward,* he thought. He could smell her flower oil perfume.

"Well, yes, I am from the mountains you could say, but I have been on the road for a while now."

"Ah, interesting. I've never met any of the cloud folk before. I heard it's pretty up there. Nice to see a calm face. Seems like nothing in this city can sit still." As she swayed away, he noticed the full curves of her body.

The master looked about the teahouse. He had been around long enough to know that not every encounter was genuine. He heard stories of women that flirted with men only to lure them to their doom. At his age, he was not accustomed to women paying much attention to him at all, never mind calling him exotic. He did not know what to think, his thoughts competing between the spark he felt from her touch and the trouble that brewed in his mind. As he looked around for her potential accomplice, no one sat in the shadows.

"Here you go, cloud man." She placed his order in front of him on a small tray. She smiled as she did so, again touching his defined arm with a little squeeze. She walked back towards the kitchen but he could feel her eyes on him. The master tried to discreetly sniff each of the ingredients on his tray. He was checking to ensure nothing was drugged or poisoned, but he sat up as he felt the woman return to his table.

"Is something wrong? Or are all you cloud folk this weird?" *This woman is quite a character,* he thought. But his order seemed to be unsoiled.

"Forgive me," he said. "I have been traveling alone for a while and you can't be too careful, especially amongst strangers." The server sat down across from him and introduced herself. Her movements were light and he caught the flowery smell of her hair again.

"There, now I'm not a stranger," she said with a girlish giggle. Someone yelled from behind them, and she looked up, before quickly getting up.

"My boss," she said. "I'll be back for you." She disappeared, the boss after her. The master hung around the teahouse for a longer time than normal, waiting for the unusual woman to reappear. But she did not. After some time, her boss returned to the table, asking if the traveler would like anything else. He appeared perturbed, seeming to want to hurry him along. The master said that he would like to thank his original server for her recommendation and the boss promised to deliver the message. Then the owner curtly saw him out, whispering roughly that the brothel was on the other side of town and that he'd come to the wrong place.

Bewildered, the master reentered the bustling street, where he met a familiar feeling he could not pinpoint precisely. He looked down the block towards his current accommodation, before turning and heading in the opposite direction. He wandered around the city streets for a while, as the sun fell behind the skyline.

In his travels, his usual habit started by settling in a place for a while, collecting some money and wares, before moving on to yet another adventure. When the money ran out, he would resettle. He was in the middle of resettling now and did not want to linger in the port city. Far too much noise and activity. He planned to leave in the next day or two to keep ahead of his expenses, which were dwindling quickly without much work. But secretly, one condition made his current standing unique, tucked away in the stout pack for safekeeping.

For the first time in a long time, the little voice that usually guided his decisions went stubbornly quiet. He learned with time that when the voice silenced, he should pay extra attention to the immediate world around him. This signal alerted him to good fortunes and bad. In the busy streets, he tried to focus and quiet his mind, running through the available options for his next relocation.

His mind remained clouded with plans until disrupted by the sounds of laughter. From the distance, he could not tell much about the two gyrating figures down the road, other than they were women, and he guessed they were drunk. They stood not far from the teahouse, outside his accommodation, and when he finally came to pass them, one woman pointed at him yelling, "There he is, that son-of-a-bitch!"

He froze, feeling the odd voice sounded jocular despite the harsh words. Both women laughed, their silhouettes pulsating as they cackled, bent over at the waist. The strange feelings that gripped him in the teahouse returned, and soon out of the dark emerged the woman who had served him earlier that day.

"This cloud man cost me my job today," she said, a bottle of liquor swinging in her hand. Inner alarms sent their first warnings. He looked around to confirm they were alone. He searched the corners for anyone waiting to pounce on him while distracted. His gaze shifted from the yelling woman to darkness and back. She came closer. Her playful demeanor from earlier in the day utterly absent.

Her eyes glowed as she raised her hands over her head, slowly swinging the bottle at his eye level. She stopped directly in front of him before tilting her head back and screaming, "Freedom!" She let out a mad laugh that reminded him of the witches in folktales. Her companion continued laughing uncontrollably, a chorus of cackles at his expense.

"Come on, cloud man, come with us," she said, relaxing her attitude, as the two drunken women headed down the road. But the master remained stationary. *What on earth was going on?* Then the little voiced peeped up just loud enough to be heard, encouraging him to follow the witchy women.

So, he did.

They walked to the riverfront, finding a soft and comparatively quiet area to sit. The women whispered and looked back at him occasionally, but despite their mysterious behavior, the master was relaxing into the situation. *Finally, a little spontaneity!*

Along the river, he sat with the two women, who continued to act in some of the least ladylike ways. They cursed, spit, and laughed like sailors, great drunken laughter that sometimes ended with curdled coughing. They finally settled down on a pair of benches at the water's edge. He sat alone, as the two women continued to look at him, whispering and chirping like girls much younger than their age. He did not find the behavior particularly becoming and started to wonder if he may be following a pair of streetwalkers. The idea made him grow uneasy again.

"What is your story, cloud man?" The question seemed to rise from the river more than the woman, but the master proceeded to share a piece of his tale: how he left the farm and studied cha in varietal practices since. He revealed how he traveled all over the countryside, to the salted shores, and through the mountains again. Then he asked his burning question.

"You two are not. . . working, are you? It's okay if you are. I'm not judging, I'm just. . . well, I just don't *do* that sort of thing." The cackling pierced the night again.

"Are you serious? So much for calling you exotic today, cloud man! I thought you just said you were traveled, but you can't even tell the difference between a lady flirting with you or a lady of the night. *My goodness!*" She snorted another laugh.

Her friend seemed weary, nudging the woman in that way. The master understood the night to be ending, and his own exhaustion became apparent. The women began to get up, but the master stayed put. He knew they would likely be headed back in the same direction, and he did not want to alert them to his resting place—on the off chance he was still considered a quarry. The night had simply been too bizarre. The women walked off, arm in arm, and it seemed over now, as they left him there on the bench. But before they got too far, the master turned and yelled, "Wait!"

The women stopped and looked back at him.

"Did you really lose your job today? If you did, I am very sorry. I do not know what I did to upset the owner, but he saw me out quite roughly."

"No, honey, it was not your fault. I was overdue for a new destination anyway. Sorry you got caught up in this." Up now and walking after them, her friend continued across the road, but the woman turned back to meet him.

"Again, if there was anything I did, I am sorry," he repeated. "I did really enjoy your selections today. Perhaps we could have tea tomorrow?" In the dark, she hid behind a casual nod, *sure.* They agreed to meet back at the riverfront the following evening.

13

HE WOKE UP TO a terrible downpour. The rains battered the mist into the ground, as walls of water saturated the earth. In the boredom of the day, he faced himself. That lady stirred so much up in a single night—*What a strange woman! Bold, forward*. He had to admit she made him feel like a leaf on the breeze, suddenly snatched out of the air. An odd feeling for a vagabond.

As the rain continued to fall, he wondered if she would be willing to meet him in such ugly weather. Not until the morning did he realize they failed to specify a particular time, just the evening. Unsure if he should head out at sunset or the late hour of their last encounter, he savored the soft mattress, knowing he would soon be back under tarp and blanket as he made his way out of the port city. He tried to remember her face, but with all the odd events and the darkness, he operated on feelings more than appearances. The spark he felt when she first touched him panged faintly.

He looked out the window of his room at a concrete wall, its solid frame outlining his entire view, as the water dripped down its solid face. His eyes softened as he began his favorite meditation technique to ease his anticipation. Slowly he inhaled, held his breath, exhaled all the way out, and then held his breath again, each for an equal amount of time. Five seconds in. . . five seconds hold. . . five seconds out. . . five seconds hold. Once that pattern was comfortable, he extended it. Six seconds in. . . six seconds hold. . . six seconds out. . . six seconds hold. Then seven. . .

When he returned his gaze to the wall, he recalled an old memory from one of the many monks encountered in his travels. When we do something healing without the presence of pain, that is when the healing energy turns to joy, to relaxation, to bliss, the monk taught. Yet we all carry some sort of pain, so we must actively heal ourselves. We cannot solely rely on external replenishment. Otherwise, we are hungry for it. We become greedy for it. Vying for resources is a natural part of life, but greediness and fear lead to destruction. Fear cannot see clearly and so only makes ugly things. That is why the concrete is often so unappealing. It is made from the fear of change, solidifying the world around us. But in time, it cracks; roots, grasses, and weeds form new settlements, and the fight for permanence continues. It is only a fight if one desires permanence. If we can adapt to the changes without attachment, then each of us plays a role in a beautiful, unfolding show. If only we could view this uncertainty with excitement!

He studied the small signs of deterioration on the concrete wall. He noted the discoloration, the small cracks, the first moss spores settling. He looked at his hands as he held them above his face. He noted the discoloration, the small cracks, the first gray hairs settling. Indeed, excitement and uncertainty began unfolding as the light faded outside his window. He put on his nicer outfit before making his way to the riverfront, his hopes high for the night out with the curious woman.

He waited for a long time. But with nowhere else to go, he stayed. He waited long enough that once he finally acknowledged his uncertainty of things, a swift deluge of inner mockery fell upon him, like a dam bursting. *What a romantic old fool I have turned into,* he thought. *A desperate old fool,* he concluded from his damp experience. In the opaque weather, unsure of what time it could be, he dragged himself back to his room, thoroughly soaked and disappointed.

His eyelids grew heavier as he laid the wet clothes out to dry, his mind filled with conflicting emotions. *What did I expect?* But expectation was not the whole story, and he loathed admitting the thought. After years of life on the road, another adventure around every corner, it finally happened. The solitude and rootlessness had caught him by the trousers. He was lonely.

Despite his weariness, he could not sleep and decided to prep for an early departure. He unearthed his stout leather pack, removing the assortment of trinkets in his care from inside, a much larger inventory now than he ever amassed before. He was calculating, and so it was unclear exactly how or when he bumped the piece of furniture, when all the treasures jumped with a clang, startling him. He looked back just in time to watch his teapot smash to the floor. *A fitting end to a stupid day*. He crashed into bed without cleaning the mess.

In the morning, his head proved clearer. He cleaned the floor of the broken pieces, which, although a disappointment, were a minor cost compared to the other treasures in his pack. He remembered a lovely teapot he saw the other night while walking and decided to head over and check if it was still available. On that note, his mood improved.

When he came upon the dark shop window, he read a peculiar notice for the early hour of the morning: *Be Back Soon*. The teapot remained on display. Without more information, the master had no choice but to wait for the shopkeeper, which took so long that his stomach growled a reminder of the far distance in which he consumed his last meal. He left the teapot and headed into an outdoor market, searching for a bite to eat and some additional supplies for the road.

He lost considerable time in the crowds, and by the time he finally returned to the shop window, a new sign stated: *Out to Lunch*. With his own lunch in tow, the master was irked at the bad timing but not put off enough to let go of the prize. He looked around for distractions and settled under one of the nearby trees, as a gust plucked a few dried leaves, sending them on a precarious descent with dramatic twists. *To be ripped away at a moment's notice, just like that,* he thought. He waited a while, walked around, and then came back to the shop yet again. This time the door was open.

All the waiting around to complete the teapot transaction cost him much of the day, but the master consoled himself with thoughts of enjoying his cha under the stars that evening. He picked up the remainder of his belongings and headed to the riverfront for a final meal before hitting the road. He sat with his back to the bustling, enjoying the only view of this city he truly enjoyed: the river. His eyes followed its curves upstream to the mountain he once called home, not too far off in the distance.

"Please don't tell me you have been waiting here since yesterday, cloud man." The odd yet familiar voice sent a shiver up his spine. He turned in disbelief, to find the strange woman walking towards him, outfitted like a traveling man. She dropped her pack and plunked down beside him with a smile. "You waited this long for me, or just staring at your relatives in the sky?"

She took in the view with a deep breath. He nodded dumbly as excitement returned to his veins. This time, he really took her in. Despite the unusual way she dressed, trousers and tunic, he could still make out the most interesting curves of her body, her full chest rising as she let out a sigh. He gawked at her, almost drunkenly.

"What are you staring at?"

He snapped back to attention.

"Sorry, I. . . I am just surprised to run into you again. I didn't think I would, when we did not meet yesterday. I was planning to head out now, but. . ." He could not finish the sentence. He was lost in her eyes.

"Yeah, I got that part," the woman said, motioning to his pack, then to her own. "Sorry I'm late. So, where are we going?" She stood up as if she was right on time and *not* coincidently running into him randomly a day later, in the precise spot they happened to agree to meet. But he wanted to have tea with the woman, so he let it go and deemed it a good fortune.

"There is a teahouse on the other side of town. We could—"

"No, no," she interrupted, "I mean, where is the next destination, cloud man? We are getting the hell out of here." She looked around, shifting her weight nervously.

Surprised, he explained, as briefly as he could, how he decided to head back up the mountain for his next adventure. He told her his journey included a night under the stars.

"Fine, sounds great, let's go. Which way?"

He pointed towards the mountain far in the distance. She let out an embarrassed sigh, slapping her forehead. "Obviously."

As they made their way out of the city, he felt curiously responsible for his new companion. He looked out for dangers not only to himself but noting each of the men taking particular notice of her. They walked along the water's edge following the flow into the woods, all the while the woman talked, at times seemingly unaware of her surroundings. Truthfully, she spoke so much that the master only caught pieces of the overall conversation, his mind wandering between focusing on the woman's oration, his inner debate on trusting her, and thoughts of where she would sleep that night.

However, in the memoir she shared with him, he caught enough to sew together that she was once married but ran away from her husband years ago. They owned a tavern. He liked the drink more than the business and began a penchant for violence as the money dwindled. One day she had enough, packed up, and disappeared. She wasn't even sure if he was still alive or drank himself to death. She didn't really think about the relationship much anymore. Like the master, she spent many recent years on the road, skipping around anytime things got stale or work dried up.

Birdsong began to replace the busy noises as the city faded into the background with the waning sunlight. By now, he thought she would have chosen her own path, but at both forks in the road they encountered, she made no move to separate from him.

"So, what actually happened that got you fired?" he finally asked.

"Oh, nothing," she said apathetically. "I never adjusted well to the decorum of the teahouses. The relaxed nature of the tavern is just in my blood. I'm always in trouble for being too kind or too casual. Men often think I am flirting with them. One time a guy got handsy and it was a problem. I think that shop owner actually thought I was using his place to arrange meetings after dark. Either that or he was into me and just jealous. I wasn't working there long anyhow."

"To be fair, you confused me," he interjected. "Are all you river women so forward?" He was teasing her, but his tone was off. She stopped and looked at him, and he stopped too. She came close to his face.

"That's different," she said. "I'm not so young anymore. When you're our age, you got to be more direct sometimes. Besides, you're a good person, I can tell." She playfully slapped him in the chest. It was hard. "I've been around long enough to be a good judge of character." She turned and began walking ahead of him.

"You must trust me to follow me into the woods at night, alone. What if I have bad intentions?" She froze at the question. She tugged at her waistband, before spinning around with a shockingly large blade.

"Well," she said calmly, dangerously calmly, "you would find out that I am not easy prey." She pointed the knife at his chest. Then she laughed her witchy laugh, sheathing the large blade in her men's trousers. "*What if I have bad intentions?*" she said in a mocking tone. "If you did, you would not be so protective of me, staring down every guy in the city that looked my way."

"Protective of you? What if I only meant to feign protecting you until we reach my desired point to have my way with you and then dispose of you in a particular place?" His voice wavered as he said it, and she cackled again, before coughing fiercely.

"Cloud man! You are such a good person, you can't even say these nasty things the right way. You would make a terrible villain. Now, you clearly are not afraid of these woods like some city boy, so where are we making camp?"

They were only a small way off a spot that he remembered well. He camped there before and could confirm its safe water access and a great view of the mountain. By the time they arrived, darkness fell. They immediately sparked a fire. As the cloud man nurtured the flames, the river woman swept out an area with her feet, kicking the debris away. He grew the fire, and she took the rope from his pack, stringing it between two trees above her freshly swept area. He made a torch and came over to hand it to her. She was stretching the tarp over the rope, pinning it to the floor with rocks at the corners.

"What are you doing?" he inquired. Only now did he notice how willingly she entered his pack.

"Setting up the tent. What does it look like?" she shot back, grabbing the torch and searching for rocks to secure the final corner. He was unsure how to raise his next question.

"Where, umm, how, uh. . ." She looked up, holding the torch out so she could see his face. The light was bright against the forest, and he could not see her, but he sputtered, "Where are you sleeping tonight?"

"In the tent obviously!" She nearly barked it.

"And where do you think I am sleeping?" he asked.

"We are sharing the tent, cloud man, but don't get any ideas. It looks like it's going to rain. I'm going to wash up. You better not follow me. Remember the blade." She clacked the metal against the torch.

He nodded, but she could not see. She headed off in the direction of the water but stopped after only a few steps when she found an open, dry area under a large tree. She began to undress by the torchlight, the flames dancing around as she switched it from hand to hand while removing her clothes. The jumping light caught his eyes, and she could not see him drinking her in, but he saw more than enough. With a symphony of soft rushing water and sounds of the night, he took in all of her in the flashes of the dancing flames. She was a river.

Under the darkness of the trees, the travelers were immersed in each other's company, unaware of the changing weather. They ate by the fireside, sitting across the flames to see each other. They joked and shared stories of their travels, of the worst people they ever met, and their favorite places. He made them cha, and she inquired into the view he had bragged about earlier.

The rain began to fall lightly as he guided her out onto the exposed rock. They barely arrived when clouds veiled the available stars and moonlight. The mountain remained hidden. He swung the torch around, searching the ground, the light waning with every drop that contacted its flames. She wondered what he was looking for when he mumbled an affirming sound, followed by a sigh of disappointment. She dragged her feet slowly through the darkness towards his dim torchlight. The master stood over a sunken divot in the rock, filled with only a small amount of water, which surprised him given the heavy rains the previous day. A dead fern withered on one end of the miniature pond.

"Last time I was here, there was a tiny world in this pool in the rock, isolated from everything else. I was hoping to show you at least something interesting since we have no moon or mountain to enjoy."

"*You're running low on luck, pal,*" the river woman said in the mocking tone. Then she hooked her arm in his. "I can't see a thing. Let's get some sleep." They walked slowly through the dark, arm in arm, back towards camp with only the torchlight to guide them.

Their fire burned low, and he reworked the flames, as the woman positioned herself inside the tent, her head facing out towards the warmth. She laid her smaller blanket as a ground cover and folded over his large blanket, sandwiching herself in between the layers. He pretended not to notice how comfortable she made herself with his things again, only alerting her that he was going to wash up. He fashioned a new torch as he said this, then headed to the water. In his absence, she applied her flower oils.

The cloud man returned quickly, stoking the fire and preparing to enter the tent. He tried to cleanse himself quickly, without alerting her to the depth of his scrubbing. It had been some time since he last shared his bed, and he felt slightly uneasy, but he dismissed it as just nerves. When he gathered himself enough to enter, she immediately noticed how nice he smelled.

"Oh, you laying on the musk for me?" she said. "I thought I said don't get any ideas?"

"And what of the flowers I smell? Those scents are not growing in the grass."

"I did that to offset the way your blanket stinks!"

She rolled over as if agitated, but he was learning how the large emotional waves were her sense of humor. He settled in with a grin and did not say anything more than "Good night." She did not respond, but almost instinctually, her body shifted closer to his.

14

WHEN THE MASTER AWOKE in the morning, he was alone. Sun trickled through the branches of the trees. He rubbed his eyes, looking around for the woman from his limited view out the tent. The fire felt strong. His back ached. It had been a while since he had slept on the ground. He slowly reached for the stout pack at his feet, but it was not there. He felt around more as panic began to rise. His pack was missing. Her belongings were missing too. There was no sign of her.

He sprung out of the back of the tent, his torpor quickly turning to rage, at himself for trusting her and at her for violating his trust. *You old fool. . .* the awful feelings were immediate and fierce, and he barely retrieved his boots, when the river woman appeared from around a tree.

"*Good morning, darling*," she said in the mocking tone. She held out breakfast to him.

"Where are my things?" he demanded, and taken aback at his harshness, she pointed under the overhang of a large rock, outside his view from the tent.

"I tucked everything over there to give us some more room and keep them out of the rain. Are you always this grumpy in the morning?" Relief hit him at the sight of the stout pack.

"Sorry," he said, shaking his head.

"Look, cloud man," she said sternly, coming into his space. "You're a man of your word, right? I'm certainly a woman of my word. I appreciate that you didn't creep on me last night, but based on how much you snore, I could have easily chopped you up." She glared at him, but he inhaled the smell of her flower oils. "I promise I won't do anything to harm you, as long as you do the same for me, okay? Can you make the same promise to me, cloud man?"

He nodded, ashamed.

"I promise," he said.

"That's settled then," she declared. "Now come look at this."

They made their way back out to the exposed rock, and the mountain was on full display. The mist circled the top of the mistress, and in the dawning light, she sparkled with all her tiny galaxies. They took in the scene for a long time, her body slowly drifting against his. He felt her curves like the river, and she let his hand wander her shores.

"*Take me to those clouds*," she said, breaking the long silence. Her tone was only half mocking now, the other half dreamy. She looked into the eyes of the man she met only a few days ago. She knew the feeling and saw it on his face the day they met too. She wanted to push it off as long as she could, to savor it. There was no guilt about her ex-husband. Time was limited. Life was limited.

She pushed herself against her travel companion, and he shifted, embracing her fully. She gazed up at the cloud man, his head wrapped in morning glow, the mountain outlining his strong figure. She knew he would be too modest, so she softly leaned into him. A familiar feeling rose in her chest, but she tried to suppress it. She wanted to fall deeper into the man, allow him to take her. Yet the feeling swelled into her throat, and before she could stop it, she broke away from his embrace, coughing violently. She apologized; he made nothing of it. But the moment passed.

Upon finally reaching the valley town at the base of the mountain, the two travelers seemed estranged. The master, thrilled to be close to home again, observed the changes during his time away. As the man bustled around, commenting, even sometimes exclaiming at the current state of the old village, the river woman ambled behind him aimlessly. The new had sprung up alongside the old and it took a moment before the master found what he was looking for, dragging her through his old, familiar streets.

Back when the master was first a steward for the visionary, he needed another job to support himself and found one as a maintenance worker for a wealthy innkeeper who owned multiple establishments. An avid collector of tea wares, the innkeeper paid a premium for antique and one-of-a-kind pieces he felt elevated his social status. The young master, being an avid cha lover but not a threat to his public standing, received most of the innkeeper's boasting about his wares, the prices he paid to acquire them, and the prices he exaggerated he could sell them for as well. The master often remained quiet during these soliloquies, allowing the innkeeper to insert his opinions when necessary, which led the collector to hold his employee in high esteem, simply for never disagreeing with him.

Now back in town, the master searched for his old boss, but the innkeeper would not return to the inn for an hour or so. The travelers dropped some of their things in a room upstairs, before washing up and heading for a nearby teahouse. They barely sat down when the master left the river woman, saying that he would be back again shortly, throwing his pack over his shoulder. He discharged before she could dispute him, and now sitting alone, the river woman wondered if she was the one being hoaxed.

This cloud man, who lingered for two days as her fate caught up to his, could not even sit still for a meal. She boiled at the lack of attention he was paying her, only long enough to rebuke herself for getting attached to a man she barely knew. But she already felt like she really understood him, and he was up to something. She finished her meal as he returned, looking very pleased. The river woman demanded an answer to the cloud man's mysterious smile, but he only told her that things were going to plan. His bag seemed empty.

The sun hung high in the sky when they returned to the inn's small room. He apologized, telling her he had more business that needed to be taken care of, leaving her again before she could say a word.

"Is this how it's going to be from now on?" she called after him, but he did not respond. She thought it better, as she immediately regretted the question.

She quickly grew bored in the confined space and wandered out into the streets. The rural town was quiet compared to the city but not lifeless. She watched small children laughing and playing. The air smelled fresh, and she strolled into a market, where many of the merchants had already gone for the day. She bought some fruit and flowers, before catching a glimpse of the sunset.

She had finally made it to the land of clouds. She took in the elevated view, much higher than she was used to, following the pastel river water from the city, upstream into the mountains it spilled from, not far off from where she stood. She spotted a narrow trail in its direction and decided to see where it would lead.

As she walked, she reviewed the recent events, now that she could think without the influence of anyone else around. She considered the cloud man, the unexpected, immediate comfort she felt with him, like they had been together forever, the way he already teased her about her big emotions, the way he was strong yet soft, *and that hard body.*

Her narrow path came to a small waterfall dropping off a sharp cut in the mountainside. The flow was not intense, but in the shallow pool below, the falling droplets crashed with offbeat sounds that unsettled her. The water screamed over the edge, and she felt every individual drop crying as it crashed below, only to be muffled again in the shallow white foam. She tried to shake it off, smelling her recently purchased flowers, drinking in the visual beauty of the wild sanctuary she stumbled upon. The pollen tickled her nose and she sneezed and then coughed ferociously. Her head spun a bit. She sat on a rock to steady herself, breathing deeply, before letting out her curdled cough.

All she could hear for a moment was her ears ringing. But as the forest returned to her, the water drops continued their cacophony. Amongst the trees and bushes, she began to see glowing eyes, an assortment of shapes and colors. Although she was frightened, they did not spark as much panic now. She recognized the sad faces of her inner fears manifesting.

They respectfully kept their distance for a long time, but with her strength declining lately, the dark creatures encircled her in the waning light. They placed their long arms around her, humming a song about how it wouldn't be long now. When the song ended, the creatures crawled back into the bushes, and she wept like a river, her tears falling into the shallow pool.

The river woman returned to the room to find it empty. She was grateful he would not see her like this. She washed for an extended period, trying to cleanse herself in the warm water. But it was no use. This could not be scrubbed away. She returned to the small room and lay down in her robe, her eyes still welling up. *Why now?* She asked the question rebelliously. She knew the answer.

The cloud man strolled in the door, washed, smiling, and carrying various items in his hands, amongst them a small bottle of liquor. This was the best mood she recalled seeing him in since they first met. As she loosely gathered herself, her sliding robe revealed additional glimpses of what he saw in the dancing flames.

"You trying to get me drunk?" she said, striving to muster her usual voice.

"Certainly not," he replied. "I've seen that show before. This is for a celebration tomorrow."

She scrunched up her face as he placed the remaining items on the dresser and removed his shoes. Then like a raucous boy, he jumped into the bed. Up close, he noticed her puffy eyes.

"What's wrong?"

"Nothing, nothing," she lied, but he could tell she was running low on her usual tenacity. They both sat up, only to lock eyes and lie back down. He put an arm around her, and her body, still warm from her bath, stiffened slightly as he held her to his chest. He yawned, and she rose and fell with his breath. He let out a sigh, a funny, relaxing sound, as he shifted them deeper into the bed.

His wonderful mood intoxicated her, dispelling any of the lingering dark creatures. He yawned again and she grew weary inside his comfort. He gathered her up, his touch soft and confident, much more so than before. She softened too. But she did not want to experience a passionate advance while still feeling haunted, and she quickly stood up, gathering a few things before declaring she would be back in a moment. She met his eyes. "Don't move," she said.

15

"THAT WAS ONE OF the luckiest days of my life." The elder smiled at the young girl and her mother. "I had been collecting wares to sell someday, perhaps even rent my own shop to do it. I wanted to see the innkeeper for a place to get started. He was my other boss while I was a steward for the visionary, and I remembered he was quite a collector. I also gave him the first pick through of my wares for his avid tea compendium. My travels had led me to some curious places, and my inventory was unique to say the least.

"When I saw him that afternoon, he bought everything I offered him! Saying that he trusted me and knew I was a man of taste from the old days. I had so much money in my pack, it made me nervous! I went back to the room I was sharing, but almost immediately, the little voice pushed me back out on the road, directly up the hill, where I saw my old cottage, still in its full glory. Well, the garden was overgrown, and the place did not seem like anyone inhabited it since my exit. . . but that was what I wished to see."

At that point, the mountain of a man and his older brother retained full control of their family's farm. When the master met with them, they were not the young boys he remembered seeing on the occasional scampering around his cottage at night. The visionary and their lion-hearted father were both deceased. The brothers recalled fond memories of the young master, of the times he saw them on their nightly adventures but never snitched to their father. He was so pleased that they had any memory of him at all, as they retold their grandfather's appreciation of his help many years ago.

"I was so touched I nearly fell over." The elder brought a hand to his heart, and the other to his forehead as if feeling faint.

"They toured me around the farm, and things had greatly changed for the better under the latest generation. My old cottage did not seem to be a part of things, and I inquired if there was any chance of my reinhabiting it." He looked around the cottage they sat in, smiling widely.

"They were not as money hungry as their father and possessed a deep appreciation for the leaves, perhaps in rebellion to his abuse of the land. Wisdom blessed them for restoring balance and harmony. Consequently, their operation was running at full capacity in their judgment. The cottage sat in the bordering lands that only served as a barrier to their interests. I offered them all the money I had, but these boys shined with their grandfather's spirit, reinstating the old terms that if I came to work for them again, I could live there rent free."

The master thanked them for their generosity but explained that he could not guarantee his working for them in the long term. He was hoping to make a more permanent arrangement, handing them the stout leather pack with all the earnings inside. The brothers looked inside to see the money, although they seemed to be more interested in the stout pack, asking about the old branding and the hand-scratched signature. He explained it was a gift from their grandfather and learned there were few family heirlooms to survive from those days.

The brothers opened the bag and checked its contents. They exchanged glances, and there was some additional muttering. They held on to the stout pack but handed a portion of the earnings back to the master. The heirloom, the money, and the fulfillment of his promise should cover the price for one small parcel of land. The older brother held out his hand for a shake to seal their agreement. As they shook, the brothers again emphasized their excitement at the master's return, keeping his promise to his old friend the visionary. A neighbor with such love of the leaves is worth far more to them than any bag of money or statue of gold, they said. To have someone else around who loved their grandfather enough to understand his vision for the ancient trees would certainly prove useful. They were close now, the clock ticking softly as the oldest grove grew another season closer towards its one-hundredth birthday.

When the river woman returned to the small room, the cloud man was exactly where she had left him on the bed but nearly asleep. *Had she been gone that long?* She had only left him for the washroom to freshen up, but perhaps she lost track of time. It was late, and she was also feeling the effects of the long day.

He lay in the middle of the bed, on top of the blankets. He looked freshened up as well, his shirt off. He was not snoring, so she concluded he could not be too deep in dreamland and debated between waking him roughly or crawling into his arms. She settled for tickling his foot, which roused him enough to open an eye. He held his arms open to her in a daze, and she climbed into his embrace before she could stop herself.

"Are you alright?" he muttered, and she wedged deeper into his hold. His hard body gently lifted her up with his breathing, and she sank into him. She wanted to tell him everything, but this was not the time. She buried herself deeper, her skin igniting against his, as more of her lay bare upon him. Her scented body filled his nose. She did not say a word. "Tomorrow will be better," he said through another yawn, and the two fell asleep without letting go.

In the morning, the river woman woke up in a high tide of blankets and pillows. She was unsure how or when she had properly gotten into bed. She reached across for the cloud man, but he was not there. She sat up to find herself alone in the small room. Her things were untouched, but all of his belongings were gone. There was no sign of him. *Ugh! I should have come on stronger,* she thought. *At least the room is paid.* She let herself drown in the sheets.

She did not awake until late in the afternoon to the smell of food, her travel companion wafting the smells over her, a plate in his hand. He was smiling broadly, telling her to eat swiftly and collect her things so he could show her what he had been doing. She shooed him downstairs to gather herself.

In the street, she looked for the cloud man, who did a little dance once she saw him. When she came close, he began to run, and she chased him like a schoolgirl, laughing and calling after him to wait so she could keep up. But the cloud man only stopped at the sight of the river woman coughing, struggling to catch her breath. He came downstream to her, but she fluffed him off, saying she was alright.

"I just ate. What are you doing to me?"

He smiled and took her pack. They walked to the outskirts up the mountain, until reaching a small cottage. A pile of fresh debris scythed from a barren garden patch sat outside by a newly swept front door. The place seemed aged. Nature crept close to its edges. The only thing that seemed new was a wooden bench placed quite intentionally, under a large tree close to the mountain road.

"*You bought me a house?*" she asked in the mocking tone. He laughed and headed for the front door. Smoke rose out of the chimney. Suddenly, the woman realized someone else may be inside. Someone like his wife. She braced for emotional impact, realizing how little she actually knew about him, as he motioned her through the open door.

Inside, it was cool and a little damp, despite the stove roasting, attempting to dry out the cottage. A candle sat on an empty table, and the fallen wax suggested it had been burning for quite some time. As she studied the tiny abode, there were many things that caught her eyes, but there was no wife inside.

"Did you do all this? When did you have time?" she finally asked, as he put a kettle on the stove.

"You have been asleep for most of the day," he said with a chuckle. "I came up at dawn. I wish it was a bit more hospitable, but I got nervous when I came to fetch you. I realized I left the candle burning. Hence the running through town."

"And here I thought you were being playful, but you were just ensuring you didn't burn *my* house down," she said with a smirk. He sat her at his empty table for tea.

"Seriously, is this your place?" the river woman inquired. He told her the full story of the innkeeper, the brothers, his new job, and if she was interested, a job for her too.

"There is very little decorum in the fields," he said with a wink. But he insisted it was only one option, since he had no idea what her intentions were now that they arrived. He completed his plan, but with no objective of imposing anything on her. Stunned and frankly flattered that he thought to include her at all, she could not believe how he actually looked out for her. But he did not calculate the realities, like where she would live or if she would be capable of doing outdoor work. Yet, as she unpacked her bag, he did not stop her.

As the blues of the sky gave way to the warm sunset, he carried a fresh teapot and two cups on a tray to the new bench, where the river woman sat underneath the large tree.

"I know this is my first day up here, but I don't think I could ever get tired of this view," she said, gazing out into the valley. "No wonder you cloud folk are so peaceful."

He smiled, pouring her cha and letting it cool as he spoke in a low, soft voice.

"From up here, you gain a different perspective. We get to watch the clouds turn into the rains, fall from the sky, run down the mountainside as individual drops, gather together and turn into the river, only to evaporate and remake the clouds. Nothing dies, only changes form. The cyclical nature of things is a big part of our lives. The same goes with the leaves. You think about the number of things that can happen over a century. Just imagine, right? And then you drink an ancient tree cha and think how each of those leaves came about *after* a century of events happened to *that* tree. It changes the flavor—young tree leaves don't taste the same. That's what I love about cha; you can settle for a cup of leaves and hot water or dig a little deeper and discover the flavor of time, steep the rise and fall of an entire universe."

He handed her the cup. They sat on the bench, looking out over the valley for a long time. It was a sight to behold, and the river woman folded herself into the cloud man. As a pastel sky gave way to the inks of night, the assortment of colorful eyes began to glow for the woman. The creatures stayed a distance away and could only look on. Perhaps they were afraid of the cloud man, and she nuzzled into him at the thought. Their eyes met, and it felt natural and easy when their lips met.

She melted, and the little voice inside him sang, so loud his ears felt like they were ringing, and everything was vibrating. His eyes remained closed, as a wave washed over her, and he opened his eyes to see the river, tears running down her cheeks.

"Don't fall in love with me, cloud man," she said through her whimpering. "I'm not going to be here much longer." She revealed to him her diagnosis and how she was already living beyond predictions. The dark creatures remained in the bushes but began to hum their song. "I ran away because I needed to see the world before I go," she said. "I didn't mean for you to get mixed up with me. When you told me you were from around here, I really just wanted a guide through the forest to the mountain. I've been slowly skipping my way here. This is the last stop."

He looked at her sternly.

"Is that all I am to you?"

"Not anymore. The first night we were supposed to meet I had a really bad day. I couldn't get out of bed and I did not have a way to contact you. I wasn't even sure where you were staying, or *if* you were staying. When I saw you at the riverfront the next day, that sure felt like fate. I mean, listen, it's been a nice little trip we've had together, but is this where it ends? You can't take care of me, and I know your type; you are going to try and make it all better, but you can't on this one," she said, her eyes welling up again as they fell from his, looking out over the valley.

"You helped me find direction these last few days," he said, taking her hand. "I have never felt so excited to be with a person. I really was not sure what would happen next for me, but with every step we have taken together, my life has fallen into a better place. Look how many things have worked out in such a short time. Seems pretty lucky."

He kissed her again. And again. He lifted her up like a child, opening the cottage doors and laying her on his bed. The river woman and cloud man poured into each other, flooding their worlds to mark the end of days. They stayed together through several cycles of the sun and moon until all of their rations were consumed, and the same needs that allowed them to stay cooped up finally forced them back into the open air.

"You can stay here as long as you like," he said, leaving for his return to the farm. "You helped me put my feet on the ground. Now I will lift you to the stars." He packed up his things and headed further up the mountain to the tea fields.

"She never left," the elder said with a smile. "But when she got really sick towards the end, I began to work less and garden more. I tried to grow the healthiest food I could for her, knowing each day I could feed her we could continue our journey together. . ." His voice trailed off. The young girl looked outside to notice his thriving garden.

"Where is your wife now?" the young girl asked. Her mother glared, red with embarrassment, kicking the young girl under the table. But the elder smiled and blew a kiss upwards to the sky.

"With the stars. But we have tea together every morning." He motioned to his post, the bench under the large tree. "I still keep the garden. And I have my fuzzy buddies." He scratched behind the ears of the skinny cat. The mother wrapped an arm around her daughter.

"We're cloud folk," said the elder. "We are survivors."

16

THE RAIN BEGAN TO let up as the old man wiped down the last teacup. He finished returning everything to its original resting place. The table serving as their classroom, sanctuary, and stage sat empty and restored to full potential. It was not long before the master began noisily clamoring about yet again, determined this time, as if he was looking for something.

"Here!" he said triumphantly, presenting the young one with a small basket. Inside contained a teapot and two cups, matching in color and size. He also gave her another small bag filled with dried fruit pieces and flowers.

"Practice with these. Now you have everything you need to become a master."

The mother and her daughter graciously bowed and thanked the elder for sharing his gifts and wisdom and agreed, should they be invited, that they would be greatly honored to join him again for tea.

As the season continued, the sun grew stronger, and the mother and her daughter enjoyed the following days with new resilience. At the sight of her daughter's excitement about cha at the master's home, the mother decided to share more of her knowledge with her daughter. Each night they prepared a routine cup of tea before sleeping, and the young girl practiced each day with the master's gifts. Her mother taught her additional tricks about changing the mouthfeel, how to gauge the temperature of boiling water by the size of the bubbles, and the different ways to steep the different-colored leaves. With the master's magic in her mind and her mother's technical precision at her fingertips, the young girl quickly became proficient at her art, although her mother always drank the cup created with cha leaves, and she remained exclusively resigned to her fruity elixir.

The festival was a great success, and the brothers orchestrated a big party for their workers and families. They cleared the desks, covered the pits with boards, and decorated the roasting house like a moon festival. The master even joined the festivities, and the young girl introduced him to the staff as the warlock, much to her amusement. But despite the cheer surrounding the celebration of the ancient tree grove, one hiccup remained: The young girl was still bound to the roasting house. Her mother did not want this to be a permanent situation, especially with the heat of summer on the way. She was admittedly unsure how she could bring up the subject to her bosses while they mingled amongst their party guests, but she hoped to leverage their jovial moods.

The young girl was ahead of her on this task and cornered the master for advice. As they discussed the problem, the master reminded her about using magic and the power of the invisible. He began to tell her a story to emphasize his point, but her eyes fixed on her mother as she chatted with the bosses. The younger brother made her mother laugh repeatedly—and not her fake, polite giggle but her true laughter. She could not hear what they were saying, but it did not seem like her release was the topic of their conversation.

An odd feeling rose in the girl, watching the mountain of a man and her mother, but it was accompanied by an even stronger feeling seeing her mother happy. Her mother seemed lighter, freer—the way she acted after a good day of gardening. The young girl knew the master's ceremony played a role in helping heal her mother. They even talked about visiting her grandfather soon. The girl was not sure exactly why, but things had been on the upswing since their tea time all together.

"Given all those details, I think you know exactly what to do," the master said, and he clapped his hands, snapping the young one out of her trance. He was smiling broadly at her. She missed the entire story. But she knew exactly what to do.

At the sight of the morning sky, a clear, empty blue, the young girl put on her most colorful sundress. Her mother inquired if she was sure she wanted to wear her nicer outfit to work, and the daughter assured her. She grabbed her recently acquired basket from the master with all its contents when they headed up the mountain.

Leaves would need some time to grow for next harvest, and many of the tasks were reduced to maintenance and repairs. The roasting house was relatively quiet and nothing was whirling in the lull after the festival.

Late in the day, the young girl revealed her basket. She placed it on the desk with a thud, hoping to catch someone's attention, channeling what the master taught her. She unfolded the cloth and displayed her teapot with its two cups. Once situated, she headed across the office to get the kettle. Her sundress was a colorful whirl, catching the eye of many of the workers, who seemed to be noticing the child for the very first time. She placed the boiling kettle on a pot holder on the corner of the desk.

She pulled her chair in and looked up to notice some of the adults looking at her, including her mother's boss, the mountain of a man. He had rarely spoken or acknowledged her directly before. Embarrassed, the girl shrank at all the attention, as the mountain pulled an empty chair up across the desk to meet the girl. He grinned a large, goofy smile to comfort her, and he motioned to begin the ceremony.

She displayed for him the fruits and flowers she intended to steep, but he shook his head. He signaled to one of the roasters, who quickly provided the boss with a small bowl of freshly prepared cha leaves. The young one studied its contents before recalling how to adjust the recipe as her mother instructed. She let the kettle cool down a bit more, while pouring some of the heated water into the teapot and cups.

The young one carried out the remaining steps she had practiced, displaying the leaves, counting as she steeped, and finally pouring the cha back and forth between the small cups. Not one drop was spilled. She handed the mountain his tiny cup with a bow.

He could not believe his eyes. The color of the liquor and the fragrant smell the leaves emitted from the cup were just right. He closed his eyes and took a sip. The mouthfeel was proper too. He was speechless, as if he just saw a magic trick. His eyes remained closed as he savored the curious moment with the young girl. Her eyes were also closed, as she sipped her first taste of real cha. She swirled the liquid in her mouth, aerating it as the master described.

When the boss opened his eyes, he saw the girl trying to contain her laughter. Confused, the boss pressed her for a review, which only made her giggle more. She admitted it was her first time trying real cha and it was not what she expected.

"It's not as bad as the smell, but it's still kind of gross," the young one said to the great delight of the adults, who were hooting at the child's honesty.

Doors opened behind the laughter, as the field workers descended upon the roasting house to clock out. Entering last, the older brother spoke with the young girl's mother until they shared a surprised look over seeing the tiny girl, sitting with the mountain of a man, huddled over a teapot for two.

He called over to them, asking if his older brother remembered when they were young and used to race, recalling their most infamous night. The older brother said he remembered his brother being a cheater with stinky feet, and they shared a hearty laugh. His younger brother reminded him what it was like being punished for one mistake, how their childhood imprisonment was far too long, and the pettiness of the young girl's crime by comparison. He smiled at the young one and declared her tenure in the roasting house complete. *This little master needs to be amongst the leaves.*

After her release from the roasting house, the young girl could not wait to run into her teacher and share the news. But with the days lasting longer, his sunrise and sunset tea were no longer crossing over with her mother's commute. She did see Bones one evening and yelled a message to him, but she concluded he must not have heard her, since the master did not answer her correspondence.

Flustered, the young girl asked her mother if they could invite the master over for tea. She happily agreed. The girl inquired if this coming weekend would be an appropriate time to extend him an invitation. Her mother blushed. *No, actually.* This weekend they would be busy, visiting her grandfather. As the plans were announced, her mother instructed the young one to pack enough for staying overnight. She spoke a bit too hurriedly, as if wanting to end the conversation before saying anything more. But the young girl sensed there was something else going on and probed for details. Her mother made her usual forceful face, signaling for the girl to quit, but her eyes shined too happily, betraying her. The girl pounced on the weakness, jumping on her mother and yelling, "Tell me! Tell meee!"

Finally, the mother confessed that the younger brother was taking her to dinner in the valley. He had asked her a few times before, and each time she declined, despite her ongoing interest. But something was different now, and after seeing him having tea with the young one, she admitted she was ready to listen to her little voice on the matter. They reviewed the calendar before settling on another date to invite their teacher, while the young one packed her bag and relentlessly teased her mother about mountain-sized smoochy kisses.

The master continued sitting at his post on the pointed peaks, waving to the locals and the travelers that passed by, smiling at the sky and enjoying his tea. He continued practicing his postures in the direction of the sun, while his cats sat on his roof, behaved mysteriously, and maintained their magical reputation in the valley. One morning, the old man came outside to find a note about his post, tied to a bouquet of beautiful vegetables:

An empty cup
A place waiting at our table
Please join us
~Jasmine

THANK YOU

THANK YOU FOR READING my story, I hope you enjoyed it over a cup or two of delicious cha. This book was a project I started during the pandemic, before finishing my first book. I was so excited to enter the world of tea with both feet that I immediately began writing about the parallels between the ways we hold space while practicing meditation and preparing tea. I read many books while the shops were closed, but by far my best teacher has been my friend Fengxiao Liu, owner of Sinofilia Tea Shop, who let me come in for tea ceremony and talked with me for hours about meditation and the practice of tea. An honest purveyor and master in the art, many of the "secrets" of this book are things she first enlightened me about. Thank you as always, my friend.

Special thanks to my production team: Mark Weinstein for your generous advice and direction; my editor David Cashion, for challenging me and making me a better storyteller; and the team at Becky's Graphic Design for making my crazy visions beautiful.

Thank you to my family, especially my wife, Casey. If you did not help so much with raising our boys, I would have no time to share my art with others. Thanks for tolerating all the impromptu ceremonies, when I know you would have rather had a cappuccino.

Thank you to all the honest purveyors who continue to educate the public about tea and its benefits. There are few things that are truly global, and maintaining cultural connections like tea are some of the best defenses we have against the political strife we suffer from currently. The tea community is a paramount example of connection through a shared passion.

Happy steeping!

MORE FROM JOHNNY

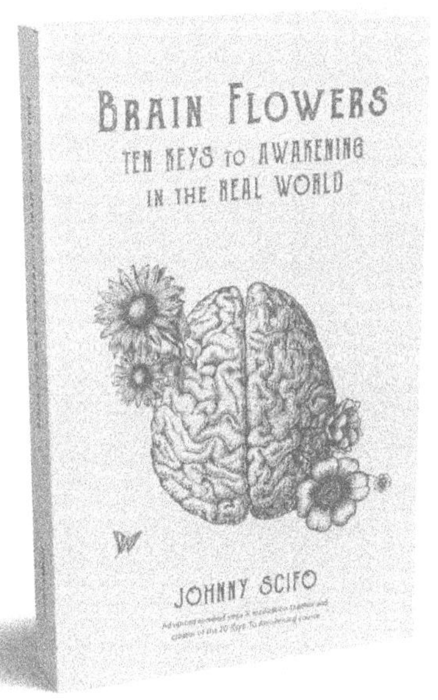

Awakening course, free meditations, and playlists at: **www.johnnyscifo.com**

www.ingramcontent.com/pod-product-compliance
Lightning Source LLC
Chambersburg PA
CBHW040905010826
48978CB00013BB/1165